Praise for
Chuck Black

"Chuck Black is a word crafter who is able to weave Kingdom principles into the fabric of one's moral imagination. The characters he has created and the passions they exude will motivate readers to follow their examples, which have now been etched into their awakened conscience."

—MARK HAMBY, founder and president of Cornerstone
Family Ministries and Lamplighter Publishing

"With sanctified imagination, Chuck Black transports readers back to the days of chivalry and valor, clashing steel and noble conflict—but ultimately he transports readers to the eternal triumph of the King who reigns!"

—DOUGLAS BOND, author of *Hold Fast in a Broken World*
and *Guns of the Lion*

"My son, Nathan, loved the first book in the series, and he said the second was even better. In my son's own words, 'Mom, it was exciting and full of mystery. It compelled me to read more. I couldn't put it down.' As a mom and an author, I give *Sir Bentley and Holbrook Court* two thumbs up!"

—TRICIA GOYER, homeschooling mom and author
of *Blue Like Play Dough*

"Chuck Black is the John Bunyan of our times! *Sir Kendrick and the Castle of Bel Lione* is a reminder of the origins of the spiritual warfare we are to fight daily."

—IACI FLANDERS, inductive Bible study teacher
and homeschooling mom

"As Christ taught in parables, you can use this powerful allegory to convey biblical truth, doctrine, virtues, and vices. Combat trained, Chuck Black makes warfare real without gratuitous violence but rather with a message of honor. Don't miss the best part: the discussion questions at the end!"

—ERIC JUDSON TIBBETS, husband, dad, and captain
in the United States Navy

SIR QUINLAN

AND THE SWORDS OF VALOR

THE KNIGHTS OF ARRETHTRAE
BOOK 5

Also by Chuck Black

SIR QUINLAN

AND THE SWORDS OF VALOR

THE KNIGHTS OF ARRETHTRAE
BOOK 5

CHUCK BLACK

MULTNOMAH
BOOKS

Sir Quinlan and the Swords of Valor
Published by Multnomah Books
12265 Oracle Boulevard, Suite 200
Colorado Springs, Colorado 80921

ISBN 978-1-60142-128-9
ISBN 978-1-60142-298-9 (electronic)

Published in the United States by WaterBrook Multnomah, an imprint of the Crown
Publishing Group, a division of Random House Inc., New York.

MULTNOMAH and its mountain colophon are registered trademarks of Random
House Inc.

Library of Congress Cataloging-in-Publication Data
Black, Chuck.
    Sir Quinlan and the Swords of Valor / Chuck Black ; [illustration by Marcella
Johnson]. — 1st ed.
        p. cm. — (The knights of Arrethtrae ; bk. 5)
    Summary: Sir Quinlan, newly commissioned as a Knight of the Prince, is brought
into an elite unit known as the Swords of Valor, but when things go wrong he is
tempted to return to his former life until a new enemy threatens and suddenly he
holds many lives in his hands.
    ISBN 978-1-60142-128-9 — ISBN 978-1-60142-298-9 (electronic)
    [1. Knights and knighthood—Fiction. 2. Good and evil—Fiction. 3. Christian
life—Fiction. 4. Allegories.] I. Johnson, Marcella, ill. II. Title.
    PZ7.B528676Skq 2010
    [Fic]—dc22

                                    2010010455

Printed in the United States of America
2010—First Edition

10 9 8 7 6 5 4 3 2 1

♛ ♛ ♛

To those who consider themselves the least…take heart,
thou mighty men and women of valor,
and be ready for God's command!

CONTENTS

KINGDOM'S HEART

An Introduction to the Knights of Arrethtrae

 Like raindrops on a still summer's eve, the words of a story can oft fall grayly upon the ears of a disinterested soul. I am Cedric of Chessington, humble servant of the Prince, and should my inadequate telling of the tales of these brave knights e'er sound as such, know that it is I who have failed and not the gallant hearts of those of whom I write, for their journeys into darkened lands to save the lives of hopeless people deserve a legacy I could never aspire to pen with appropriate skill. These men and women of princely mettle risked their very lives and endured the pounding of countless battles to deliver the message of hope and life to the far reaches of the kingdom of Arrethtrae…even to those regions over which Lucius, the Dark Knight, had gained complete dominion through the strongholds of his Shadow Warriors.

What is this hope they bring? To tell it requires another story, much of it chronicled upon previous parchments, yet worthy of much retelling.

Listen then, to the tale of a great King who ruled the Kingdom Across the Sea, along with His Son and their gallant and mighty force of

Silent Warriors. A ruler of great power, justice, and mercy, this King sought to establish His rule in the land of Arrethtrae. To this end He chose a pure young man named Peyton and his wife, Dinan, to govern the land.

All was well in Arrethtrae until the rebellion…for there came a time when the King's first and most powerful Silent Warrior, Lucius by name, drew a third of the warriors with him in an attempt to overthrow the Kingdom Across the Sea. A great battle raged until finally the King's forces prevailed. Cast out of the kingdom—and consumed with hatred and revenge—Lucius now brought his rebellion to the land of Arrethtrae, overthrowing Peyton and Dinan and bringing great turmoil to the land.

But the King did not forget His people in Arrethtrae. He established the order of the Noble Knights to protect them until the day they would be delivered from the clutches of the Dark Knight. The great city of Chessington served as a tower of promise and hope in the darkened lands of Arrethtrae.

For many years and through great adversity, the Noble Knights persevered, waiting for the King's promised Deliverer.

Even the noblest of hearts can be corrupted, however, and long waiting can dim the brightest hope. Thus, through the years, the Noble Knights grew selfish and greedy. Worse, they forgot the very nature of their charge. For when the King sent His only Son, the Prince, to prepare His people for battle against Lucius, the Noble Knights knew Him not, nor did they heed His call to arms.

When He rebuked them for their selfish ways, they mocked and disregarded Him. When He began to train a force of commoners—for He was a true master of the sword—they plotted against Him. Then the Noble Knights, claiming to act in the great King's name, captured and killed His very own Son.

What a dark day that was! Lucius and his evil minions—the Shadow Warriors—reveled in this apparent victory. But all was not lost. For when the hope of the kingdom seemed to vanish and the hearts of the humble despaired, the King used the power of the Life Spice to raise His Son from the dead.

This is a mysterious tale indeed, but a true one. For the Prince was seen by many before He returned to His Father across the Great Sea. And to those who loved and followed Him—myself among them—He left a promise and a charge.

Here then is the promise: that the Prince will come again to take all who believe in Him home to the Kingdom Across the Sea.

And this is the charge: that those who love Him must travel to the far reaches of the kingdom of Arrethtrae, tell all people of Him and His imminent return, and wage war against Lucius and his Shadow Warriors.

Thus we wait in expectation. And while we wait, we fight against evil and battle to save the souls of many from darkness.

We are the knights who live and die in loyal service to the King and the Prince. Though not perfect in our call to royal duty, we know the power of the Prince resonates in our swords, and the rubble of a thousand strongholds testifies to our strength of hearts and souls.

There are many warriors in this land of Arrethtrae, many knights who serve many masters. But the knights of whom I write are my brothers and sisters, the Knights of the Prince.

They are mighty because they serve a mighty King and His Son.

They are…the Knights of Arrethtrae!

A TALE OF TWO KNIGHTS

 There are moments in life that define who a person will be. These moments can be as precious as the gems of Alagra Briar or as dark as the caverns of Sedah, and they are as distinct and unrepeatable as the lives they have the potential to change. Unfortunately, most people fail to recognize them among the millions of other moments that make up their lives.

The moments that inspire one to greatness are authored by the King Himself. The moments that inspire one to evil are authored by the Dark Knight, Lucius. Moments of grand design are no respecter of persons, for the King has an un-Arrethtraen insistence on calling the meek and lowly to greatness as often as the noble and wealthy…and perhaps even more often.

I know this to be true, for I, Cedric of Chessington, lived through one of those moments. I received the fortuitous opportunity to choose the Prince—and define my life it did! This is not my story, however, but Sir Quinlan's story—the story of a moment in his life that reverberated across all regions of the kingdom and changed the lives of many. It is also the story of his friend and how the choice of commonality…

Well, perhaps I should just tell the tale. It begins not in the city of Burkfield, where our young Sir Quinlan lives, but in the darkened halls of evil's lair.

ONE

WORDS FROM THE DARK

 "My Lord, we nearly lost our stronghold at Moorue," Luskan reported to the Dark Knight, then turned and glared at Malco. Malco returned the glare with hatred spewing from his eyes.

The Dark Knight's fierce gaze turned toward the handsome blond Shadow Warrior. He slowly rose from his grisly throne and walked toward Malco, fingering the long dagger at his side. Malco's countenance of hatred transformed into one of terror as his master slowly circled him, stopping just to Malco's right side.

"Is this true?" Lucius leaned close to Malco's ear. "Have you nearly lost my most treasured stronghold?"

Malco swallowed hard. "No, Master Lucius. The Waters of Moorue are in full production, and I am expanding to three other cities as we speak. Lord Luskan has overestimated the importance of the skirmish in the swamp."

Luskan snorted. "The truth, my lord, is that the Knights of the Prince are purposely taking the battle to our strongholds. Malco escaped the fate of Drox by the hair of a blood wolf."

Lucius stood straight and walked away, then turned to face Malco with a voice thick with anger. "I have given you more warriors, Vinceros, and resources than any of my other lieutenants."

Lucius closed the space between them and drew his knife. Malco worked to keep his face stoic, but his eyes betrayed him.

Lucius put his left hand on Malco's shoulder and gripped it tightly. He raised his dagger, positioned the tip of it beneath Malco's left eye, and pressed until a bright red trickle spilled down Malco's cheek. Slowly Lucius drew the blade downward, slicing the fair skin of Malco's face.

Malco winced but stood still as Lucius spoke in a deep, guttural voice. "Do not fail me, Malco, or this blade will cut more than your pretty face!" He stopped the blade just above Malco's lip, then withdrew it and turned away.

Malco lifted a hand to cover the bloody gash. "Yes, my lord," he said in a voice full of fear and loathing. He turned and exited the hall.

Lucius returned to his throne and scowled as he gazed at nothing. Luskan stayed silent, waiting for the brilliant mind of his dark master to formulate a counteroffensive to the attacks of the wretched Knights of the Prince. After a long silence, Lucius spoke.

"The Rising is close. I can feel it!" Lucius clenched a fist. "We need something that will strike at the heart of His knights—something they cannot see nor fight, that will kill them before they know it." Lucius's fingers drummed on the arm of his throne as he turned to his vice commander. "Bring Lord Pathyon to me."

Luskan looked hesitant.

"Bring him now!" ▨

TAV AND TWITCH

 Unlike many cities in Arrethtrae, Burkfield was a place of peace, comfort, and prosperity. Nestled among beautiful low hills, it had grown from village to town to city in short order. The shops were quaint, the streets clean, and the people friendly and hospitable.

The bell tower, set upon a rise near the city center, served as a daily reminder to all who lived there that life was good for the citizens of Burkfield. All civic activities took place in the buildings surrounding the bell tower, and the square nearby was the prime location for citywide celebrations and festivities.

The city leaders prided themselves on their progressive spirit. All orders and guilds that supported the city statutes and promoted its excellent reputation were welcome, and all who loved peace were universally accepted.

Accordingly, the Knights of the Prince had encountered little resistance in establishing a thriving haven in Burkfield. The haven leaders found it reasonably easy to recruit men and women into its ranks, for without threat of persecution they could promote the cause of the Prince openly. Young people were especially eager to join and learn the art of the sword. Much of the haven's resources went toward training camps for the young knights who would eventually be commissioned to embark on their own missions into the kingdom for the Prince.

"Twitch, why don't you train the recruits in the sword today?" Tav said with a smile. He swiped his hand back through his wavy brown hair, revealing the confident blue-eyed gaze of a sturdy young man.

"I don't think so, Tav," his friend replied. "They deserve someone who really knows what he's doing."

"Look, the best way to get better at something is to teach it." Tav put a strong hand on his friend's shoulder. "You can do this." He swung his sword in a powerful arc and deftly brought its tip to the top of his scabbard, then smartly snapped it in place. "Besides," he said as he pointed to a nearby group of young men and women, "I've already told them you'd be their instructor, and they're waiting for you."

"Gee, thanks," Twitch muttered. A muscle in Twitch's right cheek jerked involuntarily, and he reached up to massage it with his right hand. His auburn hair framed a tender face that was in the final process of losing its boyish look.

"All right," he finally said. "I'll give it a try. But you'd better be ready to jump in if I need you."

Tav slapped Twitch on the back. "I'm there for you, chum."

Twitch was a year younger and a full two inches shorter than his sturdy companion, but that didn't matter—Tav and Twitch were the best of friends. Like salt and pepper, they were rarely seen apart.

They had been close even before the tragic death of Twitch's parents nine years earlier, an event that strengthened the bond of brotherhood between them. Tav's parents had taken Twitch into their home and raised him as their own, for he had no living relatives to help him. Because of his slight stature and his facial tic, Twitch proved an easy target for bullying, but Tav made sure it never happened, at least not while he was around.

At fourteen and fifteen, the two boys had joined the Knights of the Prince and begun their training together. Though Tav found it much easier to master the necessary skills, Twitch kept trying, and Tav helped him. Now at nineteen and twenty, both were on the verge of being commissioned.

Twitch walked over to the new recruits and introduced himself.

After a few stammered words, he paired up the recruits and began a series of drills. Despite his apprehension, the training session went reasonably well. The recruits were so new and inexperienced that he was able to stick to the basics of sword fighting for the whole session.

"You did well, Twitch," Tav said as they walked to the stables to retrieve their horses, Valiant and Kobalt.

"Thanks." Twitch sheathed his sword and shot Tav a smirk. "But if you're going to do that to me again, give me a little advance warning, will you?"

Tav laughed. "If I did, you'd never agree to it."

Twitch shrugged. "I suppose you're right."

"And I'm right about this too," Tav said with his trademark grin. "It's time to head for the lake."

The haven of Burkfield lay on the northeast edge of the city, next to the river that flowed south to Daydelon. Due west stood the Emerald Hills, a submountainous region that was a picture of absolute beauty, especially in the morning when the first rays of sunlight broke upon their eastern faces. Mount Resolute, the crown of the region, seemed to bask in the adoration of the lesser hills. Jewel Lake, nestled near the mountain's base, was a favorite destination for Tav and Twitch. They often enjoyed hunting and fishing there after training at the haven.

Although they hadn't planned on fishing today, the bright blue sky and the cool breeze offered an invitation they couldn't refuse. Before an hour had passed, they were casting their lines into the sparkling water, hoping to catch some of the delicious brown trout that populated the lake.

"Are you going to see Mirya again tonight?" Twitch reached for a worm.

"I guess I'm looking for an excuse to go see her," Tav replied. "Hey, she's got a younger sister. Why don't you come along?"

"Ah, I don't think so. That's just not something—"

"Why didn't I think of that earlier? You'd have a great time."

"No, *you'd* have a great time. *I'd* have a lousy time." Twitch's right cheek had begun to convulse as the conversation progressed.

"I insist, chum," Tav pressed. "Come for just a while. You can leave whenever you like."

Twitch hesitated.

"It's settled, then." Tav smiled. "We'll take our catch home, clean up, and make a visit."

"Why do I let you talk me into such things?" Twitch shook his head and recast his line.

"Because if I didn't, you'd sit around like moss on a rock." Tav jabbed Twitch's shoulder.

"I really don't like you. I hope you know that," Twitch grumped.

"Yep." Tav flashed a grin. "I know it."

"Tav, have you decided what you're going to do once you're commissioned. I mean, are you set on staying in Burkfield?"

Tav looked across the lake, gazing at the rippling reflection of Mount Resolute. "I'm not sure yet."

"You're one of the best that's ever been through training," Twitch said.

Tav shook his head, trying to refuse the compliment.

"It's true," Twitch continued before Tav could say anything. "I heard Sir Carter and Sir Urak talking. They have high hopes for you."

"We joined the Knights of the Prince nearly five years ago." Tav cast his line gently into the lake. "Now I look at the older knights who work at the haven, and I watch the knights on missions come and go, and I can't help but wonder, is there something more to following the Prince than this? Do you ever wonder that, Twitch?"

Twitch opened his mouth to speak, but just then Tav's line jerked, and soon he was occupied with bringing in a nice-sized brown trout. Then Twitch's line jerked, and they became lost in the joy of a bountiful catch, never returning to finish their conversation about the Prince and their future with Him.

"I will never let you talk me into such a thing again," Twitch complained that evening as they rode home from Mirya's house.

"Oh, come on. It wasn't that bad, was it?"

"I'd rather smash my thumb with a hammer," Twitch replied sternly.

Tav shook his head. "All right, chum. I won't force you again. When it comes to women, you are on your own."

By now the sun was set and the street lanterns were lit. Tav and Twitch turned the corner off the main thoroughfare of the city and entered a merchant street that earlier had been full of people working and purchasing goods. Now the shops were dark and locked up…all but one. Its door was open, and yellow lantern light spilled onto the street. Inside they could hear the shopkeeper's cheerful whistle.

As Tav and Twitch passed by, the merchant gave them a friendly wave. They saluted and carried on their way. Tav glanced back at the shop once more, then reined in Valiant.

"Twitch, look!" Tav pointed back at the merchant's shop.

On the counter of the merchant's shop stood the strangest little creature either of them had ever seen. The tall, bald-headed merchant stopped whistling long enough to speak softly to the animal, then put his hand on the counter next to it. It scampered up the merchant's arm and onto his shoulder.

"You're welcome to take a closer look," the merchant called out.

Tav looked at Twitch and shrugged. They dismounted, sauntered into the shop, and approached the counter. As they came, the little animal began to make soothing, chortling sounds in its throat.

The closer they came, the more amazed they were at what they saw. The furry gray and black creature, about the size of a large hand, scurried back and forth from one shoulder of the merchant to the other. It was as quick as a tree squirrel and as nimble as a monkey, with large, captivating dark eyes, a kitten nose, and dexterous little paws that worked like hands. A furry tail two-thirds the length of its body swished from side to side, helping it keep its balance.

Tav and Twitch couldn't help but smile as they watched the little animal. It lifted itself high on the merchant's right shoulder to get a better look at the knights, then flitted back down the merchant's arm to stand in front of them.

"What in the kingdom is it?" Tav asked.

The creature tilted its head to the side as Tav spoke, then made its throaty chortling noises as if to respond to his question. Tav laughed and put his hand out to the critter. It sniffed his finger, then rubbed the back of its head against his hand much as a purring kitten would do.

"This is the rare and exquisite paysonomus thapira, commonly known as a paytha," the merchant said proudly. "There isn't another merchant in all of Arrethtrae who can get his hands on one of these. You two are the first to see this little guy. I'm sure it will be gone as soon as I open my door tomorrow morning."

By now the furry little paytha had crawled up Tav's arm and was flitting from shoulder to shoulder, seeming to enjoy its new perch. At one point it stopped near Tav's neck and snuggled under his chin. Tav gently removed it and held it toward Twitch. Twitch stroked the back of its neck and it chortled warmly.

"I think the paytha likes you. These little guys are extremely intelligent," the merchant continued. "You can train them to fetch just about anything you want, as long as they can carry it. And once they know what you like, they will remember it forever."

"How big will he get?" Twitch asked.

The merchant nodded and smiled. "Good question, sir, good question. The answer is…as big as you want it."

Both Tav and Twitch looked at the merchant quizzically.

"What?" Tav asked.

"These little critters can survive on almost nothing. A few kernels of corn a day would keep this little guy happy forever. But if you feed it more, it will never get fat—just bigger. You might want to train it to fetch your shoes or how to hunt—"

"Hunt?" Tav and Twitch asked simultaneously.

"As I said"—the merchant nodded toward the paytha, which was now sniffing the air and looking off into the distance—"this animal is extremely intelligent. To do a task that you'd like it to do, simply feed it until it's big enough to do it."

"Mirya would love this little guy," Tav said. "How much is he?"

"The paytha's not for sale," the merchant said.

Tav and Twitch looked straight at the merchant for the first time. His dark eyes and pleasant smile gave the impression you could tell him anything, just like a real friend.

"What do you mean?" Tav said, disappointed. "I thought you said the paytha would be gone first thing in the morning."

"I did and it will, but it's not for sale," the merchant said. "My trade agreement with the supplier won't allow a monetary exchange." Then a broad smile crossed his lips. "But I can trade for it."

Tav smiled back and reached for a pocket in his doublet, but the merchant held up a hand.

"Keep in mind, sir, this is a rare creature. Its worth is significant."

Tav stopped, then reached for the gold necklace that hung about his neck. He removed it and held it out to the merchant, who examined it and handed it back.

"That looks like a fine piece, indeed, but I'm afraid I cannot accept it." The merchant slowly shook his head and pointed toward the back wall of his tiny shop. "My specialty is armor and weaponry."

Along the back wall hung a variety of highly polished pieces—breastplates, helmets, shields, vambraces, gauntlets, and swords.

"In this region of the kingdom, especially in Burkfield, there's really not much of a market for the extra armor, so I export these pieces to other regions of the kingdom to those who truly need them. Now, if you were to have something along this line, we could talk. Otherwise"—the man yawned—"I am quickly tiring and must get some sleep soon."

The merchant put his hand on the table and tapped. The paytha jumped from Tav's palm and ran to the merchant's hand, then scurried up his arm.

Tav pushed his hair back, thinking quickly. "I have my leather vambraces. Would they do?"

"I'm afraid not, sir. Tomorrow I am certain I'll have a dozen offers for excellent shields, helmets, and even swords."

The merchant reached for the shutters to close up the shop window. The paytha looked sadly at Tav, dropping its chin on the merchant's shoulder much as a sad puppy would do.

"Wait." Tav held up his hand. He took off his vambraces and set them on the table. "Consider this a down payment—and I'll be here tomorrow morning with my shield."

Twitch looked at Tav. Tav looked back at his friend. "I haven't used it for months, not even in training."

Twitch stayed silent.

"How do I know it isn't some rusted-out chunk of iron?" The merchant picked up the vambraces and examined them.

"It isn't. I'm a Knight of the Prince."

The merchant stared at Tav and finally nodded. "Very well, then." He held out his hand.

"How do we know this little guy won't run away the first day he has him?" Twitch asked.

The merchant looked at Twitch with a sparkle in his eye. "Because I'll guarantee the deal. I'll keep the shield here in my shop on the back wall. If you aren't completely satisfied with your critter for any reason, bring him back, and I'll return your shield to you."

Tav looked at Twitch and raised an eyebrow, then smiled at the merchant and shook his hand.

They left the merchant's shop and mounted up to ride home, eager to return the next morning and finish the deal.

THREE

DISTY AND BLI

Tav had fully intended to give the cute little paytha to Mirya, but after two days with the animal, he just couldn't give it up.

"What's his name?" Twitch asked one evening as Tav tried to teach the paytha how to fetch a nail for him. They were in Tav's father's carpentry shop, putting tools away for the day. Tav tapped the shop bench, and the paytha scurried down his arm onto the hard surface. Tav held the nail in front of the little creature.

"I think I'll call him Disty."

Twitch laughed. "That's a strange name, but it sure fits him."

"Nail," Tav said, and gave it to Disty. Disty held the nail in his little hands and sniffed it. He turned it over a couple of times, then set it down, looked up, and chortled as if to say, "I get it."

Tav grabbed the nail, walked to the end of the bench, and put the nail into the proper bin. He came back, stood by Twitch, and commanded, "Disty, get the nail."

Disty tilted his head to one side, chortled, and scurried down the bench. He hunted about for a few seconds, found the bin, grabbed the nail, and scurried back to Tav. He set the nail down, then scampered up Tav's arm to sit on his shoulder.

Twitch's mouth dropped open. "That's impossible!"

Tav smiled broadly. He quickly set to work teaching Disty to fetch other tools, but the paytha was too small to carry most of them.

That night Tav fed Disty a delicious supper of corn cakes and carrot greens. The next morning, they were almost certain he was a little bigger. And within two weeks Disty had doubled in size. He was able to carry some of the heavier tools that he couldn't carry before. And he proved every bit as intelligent as the merchant had said, and more so.

"That animal is scary smart," Twitch said as he and Tav rode to the haven one day. Disty perched high on Tav's shoulder enjoying the excursion. It had been a full week of work at the family carpentry shop where Tav and Twitch worked, and this was their first chance to resume their training.

"We should see if the merchant has any more paythas for trade," Tav said. "You ought to get one, chum. As soon as this one gets a little bigger, I'm going to teach him how to hunt."

Twitch laughed. "Teach him to fish… Then I'll consider it."

Tav raised an eyebrow. "Now that's not a bad idea."

Disty was a big hit at the haven. Some of the knights teased Tav at first—until he showed them how smart the animal was. Then training all but came to a halt, and Disty entertained the entire haven for most of the evening. When it came time for Tav to train some of the newer knights in sword, he commanded Disty to wait on a nearby fencepost, but Disty whimpered until Tav allowed him to perch on his shoulder. This hindered Tav's swordsmanship to a degree, but the trainees didn't mind. They were completely enamored with Disty. Each took turns petting the paytha and enjoying the creature's antics.

By the middle of the next week, two other knights had paythas. When Sir Edmund, the haven leader, saw the animals were becoming a distraction, he restricted their presence at the haven. Tav and the other knights argued that the paythas could be useful and promised not to let them interrupt the training, but Sir Edmund did not yield.

One morning after the fourth week, Tav woke up to quite a surprise.

"Twitch, quick, come here!"

Twitch entered Tav's room to see him kneeling on the floor beside Disty's blanket. Right beside Disty was a thumb-sized paytha curled up in a little ball. Disty looked up proudly at Tav and Twitch, then turned and licked the little creature.

Twitch blinked and shook his head. "I thought Disty was a male."

"So did I," Tav said. "I think we need to pay a visit to that merchant."

"I never said the paytha was either a male or a female," the merchant said as he straightened a few items on a shelf. "The fact is, it's both."

"What?" Tav and Twitch said simultaneously. Both wore a look of disgust.

The merchant looked over his shoulder at them. "Paythas are both male and female—or neither, however you want to look at it."

"So he…she…it was pregnant when you sold it to me?" Tav said.

"No, of course not." The merchant came over and rested his elbows on the counter. "And I didn't sell it to you." He held up a finger. "I traded with you, and I never trade a pregnant paytha. That could be dangerous."

Tav squinted at the man with a pained look. "Look, mister, I've only had the critter a little over four weeks. How can it reproduce that quickly?"

The merchant folded his hands and brought two fingers up to his lips, seemingly pondering the question. "That is quite remarkable, I must say, but not unheard of. You see, once paythas reach a certain size they can reproduce, especially if they sense other people are enjoying them too. Have you taken yours to be with other people?"

Tav and Twitch stared at each other.

"Look." The merchant pointed to Tav's shield on the wall. "There is your shield, just as I promised. You can exchange your paytha for the shield right now if you like. But the way I see it, you just doubled your investment."

The corner of Tav's mouth curled up. "It's all right. I'll keep the paytha. I just wanted to know what had happened."

"Very well, then." The merchant winked. "You gentlemen have a great day."

Tav and Twitch left the shop and continued on their way to the haven.

"Twitch, the little one is yours if you want him—er, it," Tav said.

"Are you sure?" Twitch asked. "I thought you might give it to Mirya."

"I think you would enjoy it more, if it's as smart as Disty." Tav grinned. "I can't wait to see what Disty can do on a hunting trip."

Twitch smiled as he thought of it. "Fresh game every night... Thanks, Tav."

A few days later, the new paytha, now grown to palm size, was perched on Twitch's shoulder, making high-pitched chortles.

Tav chuckled as Disty talked back to the little creature from Tav's shoulder. Disty's sounds were deeper, but still every bit as comforting to hear.

"What are you going to call it?" Tav asked.

"His name's Bli." Twitch stroked the back of the paytha's little head.

Tav laughed. "That's a strange name, but it sure fits."

Within a month, Bli was big enough to keep up with Disty. Tav and Twitch taught the two paythas how to hunt, and they seemed bred for the task, with keen eyesight and an uncanny sense of smell. The little animals made every activity outside the haven twice as enjoyable as before. They also continued to reproduce. Before long, in fact, nearly all the younger trainees and many of the older knights at the haven owned paythas, and those who didn't envied those who did. Sir Edmund was at a loss as to what to do, even though the quality of the training declined.

"Hey, Twitch, what do you say we take Disty and Bli fishing after work to see what they can do?" Tav said one day during their noon meal.

"But we have a training session at the haven tonight," Twitch half protested.

Tav swallowed a bite of food and nodded.

"Sure would be nice to have some fresh fish for dinner," Tav's mother said as she sat down at the table.

"Aren't you going to be commissioned soon anyway?" Tav's father put a succulent piece of venison into his mouth. "I'm ready for you two to be done with your training so we can get on with business. I've given up far too many jobs because of that haven."

"I get commissioned next month," Tav said. "Sir Edmund has asked what my plans are."

Tav's parents quit chewing their food and stared at him.

"Don't tell me you're planning on running off on some wild nonsense adventure." Tav's father said. "Your uncle Baylor did that, and we've barely heard from him since."

"I knew this was a bad idea from the beginning," Tav's mother added.

Tav glanced over at Twitch, both remembering their decision to become knights. It had actually been Tav's idea to join, but both boys had accepted the Prince's story gladly. Back then, the prospect of serving the King on grand missions had seemed exciting and appealing.

Those days seemed a hundred years ago now.

"I really do think Disty and Bli would enjoy fishing," Tav said to Twitch. "Don't you think we could skip training just for the night?"

Twitch shrugged and nodded. It was becoming tiring to work all day and then train in the evening too.

Less than an hour after putting away their tools for the day, they were at the lake, enjoying the late afternoon sunshine and laughing at the antics of the paythas, who picked up the concept of fishing even more quickly than they expected. When Tav snatched the first fish out of the water, the two critters jittered about excitedly. They ran up and down the shoreline, searching the waters, then stopped and chatted back to Tav and Twitch. The men cast in their lines.

It was the best two hours of fishing they'd ever had.

Life was good… Life was easy.

FOUR

MOUNT RESOLUTE

"What is this all about, Tav?" Twitch said, breathing hard. "Who is this man you're supposed to meet?"

Tav crested the last rise on Mount Resolute and held his hand down for Twitch to grab hold of. "He's my uncle."

"Seriously? The one your father's not so fond of?"

"That's the one."

Twitch clambered up over the rise and let out a low whistle. "Whenever Baylor comes by, things get tense around the house. It's a good thing it's only once in a blue moon."

Tav looked about the small clearing where they stood. From here they had a clear view of the peaceful city of Burkfield. Somewhere in the trees below them were their horses and the paythas, who had reluctantly obeyed orders to stay behind.

"You're right about that." Tav took a deep breath. "It's why my parents were hesitant to let me join the Knights of the Prince. They consider my uncle a little crazy."

"Why?" Twitch asked.

"Because I believe that following the Prince requires sacrifice," a deep voice boomed from behind them.

Tav and Twitch jumped and whipped about.

"Uncle Baylor," Tav said without smiling.

"Hello, Gustav."

Sir Baylor was a broad-shouldered man with black hair and a short black beard that was just beginning to fade to gray near his chin. Most of his knightly attire was black or dark brown leather. He cast a quick scrutinizing glance over both young knights but then focused on Tav. "I'm glad you decided to come. I thought perhaps your father had persuaded you to the contrary."

Tav stiffened. "My father doesn't know I'm here. I'm my own man now."

Sir Baylor squinted and lifted a gloved hand to his chin. "Yes, I can see that. Sir Edmund tells me you have done very well in your training. You don't know this, Gustav, but I've been checking up on your progress this past year, which is why I wanted to meet with you privately… Hello, Twitch."

Twitch's right cheek jerked a couple of times as he nodded a greeting.

"Why did you want to meet with me, Uncle Baylor?"

Baylor's eyes narrowed as his gaze returned to Tav.

"What are your plans when you are commissioned?"

Tav looked off to the woods. "I hadn't thought about it much. For now, I guess I'm planning on staying in Burkfield."

Baylor looked disappointed. "Why?" he asked bluntly.

Tav seemed a little agitated. "Burkfield's a great city. We have a good business, and I have a lot of friends here."

"Comfortable, are you?" Baylor asked.

Tav eyed his uncle suspiciously. "Yes…"

Baylor put a hand on Tav's shoulder. "Do you understand what it takes to truly follow the Prince?"

Tav squirmed and glanced at Twitch, who was closely watching the exchange.

"Of course I do," Tav replied.

"Tav, there is a war raging all around us." Baylor's hand tightened on Tav's shoulder. "I want you to come with me, to help me fight it. I'm looking for knights who are willing to ride far, fight hard, and sacrifice everything for the cause of the Prince. Such a life is not easy, but it is full of purpose. Aren't you looking for more purpose than a comfortable living and a few friends?"

Tav seemed to struggle for the right words. He walked a few paces toward the ridge line, then turned back.

"I hardly even know you, Uncle Baylor, and I'm not sure what you're asking of me."

Baylor smiled. "I'm asking you to give up everything you know here, travel from one end of the kingdom to the other, and carry the truth of the Prince to all people."

"And we would leave right after my commissioning?"

Baylor hesitated. "Unfortunately, I can't wait that long. It may be months before I return. We would leave the day after tomorrow."

"Day after tomorrow?" Tav's eyes widened. He stared at his uncle, then at Twitch. Finally he shook his head. "I have to think about this."

Baylor frowned. "I'll be here for the next two evenings if you choose to follow." The veteran knight began walking toward the tree line. "Gustav, you should know that I am not here simply because you are my nephew. I was sent for you."

The two men locked eyes; then Baylor disappeared into the woods.

Twitch came to stand by Tav, who seemed lost in thought.

"Come on, Twitch," Tav finally said. "Let's get out of here."

That night neither Tav nor Twitch slept well, and their paythas seemed as agitated as they. In the morning the two young men worked in near silence. When they finished early, Disty and Bli scurried over to their fishing rods and chortled excitedly. Much to the creatures' disappointment, however, Tav and Twitch went to the haven instead.

Late in the afternoon when the training ended, Sir Edmund gathered all of the knights and gave an impassioned speech on the need for each of them to commit fully to the Prince's call. On the way home, neither Tav nor Twitch broached the subject of Sir Edmund's speech or the previous day's encounter with Sir Baylor.

The next day was much the same, but instead of going to the haven, they arrived home for an early supper. Afterward, Tav went to the barn and began to saddle Valiant. Twitch followed him, his right cheek in near constant spasms.

"What're you gonna do, Tav?" He rubbed his cheek to soothe the muscles. Disty and Bli chortled back and forth, seeming to console each other for their masters' apparent distress.

Tav cinched and buckled his saddle, then leaned against his horse and crossed his arms. Disty scurried up to his shoulder.

"I honestly don't know, Twitch. What do you think about it all?"

Twitch's eyebrows raised. "I…well…I guess I'm not sure."

"My folks would have a fit if they knew I was even considering riding off with Uncle Baylor." Tav shook his head as if he could imagine it, then gave Twitch a crooked smile. "Do you think my uncle is crazy? I mean, do you see any sign of a war raging around us?"

Twitch raised an eyebrow. "Well…"

"Me, neither. Why should I throw everything away to chase some crazy war concocted in the mind of my uncle? I think my father may be more on track about Uncle Baylor than I first—Disty, calm down. It's all right."

Tav reached up to pet the paytha, which was running excitedly from shoulder to shoulder. Then he shook his head again and reached for the reins of his horse. "He said we may not be back for months! How would I explain that to Mirya? She's not going to wait around for me indefinitely."

"You don't really think your uncle is crazy, do you?"

Tav looked at Twitch and thought for a moment. "I guess not. I'm just not ready to accept his version of what it means to be a Knight of the Prince."

Tav prepared to mount Valiant, but Twitch grabbed his arm.

"Do you remember when you asked me if I thought there was something more to being a Knight of the Prince than what we were doing here at Burkfield?"

Tav looked at Twitch and slowly nodded.

"Do you think this could be it? What if your uncle is offering the very thing you were looking for?"

Tav seemed stunned by Twitch's questions. He looked out the barn door for a long moment, contemplating the two futures his next action would bring. "If it is," he finally said, "I guess I'm just not ready to commit to it yet." He smiled. "Besides, what would I do without you to keep me in line?"

Tav mounted up and settled into the saddle. "I'm meeting up with Mirya for an evening ride," he said. "You're welcome to come, Twitch." Disty chortled excitedly, seeming to anticipate an evening of fun.

Twitch smiled sheepishly and shook his head. "Thanks, but no thanks." Bli rested his chin on Twitch's shoulder and chortled in low, somber tones.

Tav nodded. "I'll see you later, then. By the way," he said with a wink, "there's more to you than most people think."

Twitch patted the horse's rump as Tav trotted off. He walked out of the barn and looked up to Mount Resolute, where his mind had been all day long.

"Something more…," he murmured. Bli's ears perked up as Twitch turned and headed for Kobalt's stall.

FIVE

DEFINING MOMENT

 Twitch could hardly remember life without Tav. In fact, Twitch had never made any significant decision without first consulting his confident and sturdy friend. He almost felt as though he was betraying Tav when he rode alone to Mount Resolute that evening.

I doubt Sir Baylor will even talk to me once he realizes that Tav isn't coming, Twitch thought.

All through the ride, he kept second-guessing himself. Once he even stopped and considered turning back, but something deep within kept driving him forward.

Bli seemed excited at first to be out with Twitch, but as they neared the base of Mount Resolute, the paytha began to flit nervously from shoulder to shoulder. At one point the little claws grabbed so tightly that Twitch had to stop. "It's all right, Bli," he told the paytha in a soothing voice. "Nothing's going to happen to you."

That helped until they reached the base of Mount Resolute, where Twitch tied Kobalt to a tree. He tried to make Bli stay with the horse, but the paytha wouldn't leave his shoulder. Finally Twitch gave in and let Bli ride on his back as he climbed once again to the clearing atop the mountain.

Twitch reached the crest and walked into the clearing, feeling vaguely unsettled. He looked about for Sir Baylor, but all that moved were tree branches stirred by the cool evening breeze, so he sat down on a large rock and waited. Bli scurried down his arm, then jumped to the ground to forage for insects. Twitch watched the paytha for a long while, then finally decided he must have missed Tav's uncle.

As he prepared to leave the clearing, the setting sun captured his attention. The gentle breeze dissipated as if to give the glowing orb center stage for the day's finale. Streams of sunlight seemed to beckon across the sky, and Twitch wished he could follow. For some reason his heart ached. Sir Edmund's passionate plea to be serious about serving the Prince and Sir Baylor's call for Tav to take up a mission of purpose had stirred his soul, and he could not remain still. He slid from the rock and fell to his knees.

"My Prince…," Twitch began, but Bli scampered over and leaped up onto his chest, chortling in a low angry tone. Twitch gently pushed the creature back to the ground, but Bli dug his little claws through Twitch's tunic and into his skin.

"Hey!" Twitch shouted. Normally this would have sent Bli cowering to a corner someplace, but not this time. The paytha scurried right up his chest and over his shoulder, then latched onto his back.

"Bli, get down." Twitch reached over his head for the paytha, but the sharp claws dug in deeper. Twitch squeezed Bli just enough to let him know he was serious. Bli responded by biting Twitch's thumb.

"Ouch!" Twitch yanked his hand away. Blood was trickling down his hand. "What is wrong with you?" he said angrily.

Bli's chortles became low growls. "Get down!" Twitch ordered again, but Bli just growled more loudly.

Now Twitch was getting nervous, fully expecting the animal to chomp into his unprotected neck. He reached back again, and this time the paytha didn't even wait for Twitch to grab him before biting the fleshy skin between his thumb and finger. One of the paytha's hands reached around and sank sharp claws into Twitch's right cheek. Twitch reached with his other hand and grabbed the creature by the back. As he yanked it away, Twitch felt the paytha's claws rip small pieces of flesh from his shoulder, back, neck, and cheek. At that point, the creature turned into a snarling, wild-eyed beast.

"Bli!" Twitch shouted, trying to bring the animal to its senses, but it bit and clawed at Twitch's hands until he was bleeding from a dozen places. Twitch finally threw the animal away from him and drew his long knife. Bli hit the ground and immediately turned back toward Twitch. It snarled as it flicked its tail from side to side, apparently looking for the right moment to attack. Twitch stood up, and that seemed to cause the paytha to hesitate. Then it froze, perked up its ears, and scurried off into the woods.

Twitch was breathing hard, and his heart was racing. He took a moment to catch his breath, watching and waiting for another attack from the paytha, but it did not come. Finally he sheathed his knife and dabbed his bleeding wounds on his tunic, wondering what had happened. The only other time the paytha had ever growled was once when Sir Edmund came near to talk at the haven.

Rattled by Bli's sudden vicious behavior, Twitch took a deep breath and turned to leave, but the beauty of the sunset once again captured his attention. His mind took some time to clear, but he felt better with each passing moment. Strangely, it felt good to have his shoulders free from the weight of the paytha, and his mind finally seemed at peace without the animal's constant chortling. He felt…free, and his thoughts turned once more to the Prince. He knelt down.

"I haven't much to offer, my Prince, for I am unskilled, ill-equipped, and unworthy." Twitch opened his hands and spread his arms out before him. "Yet I offer myself to You. If there is something more to following You, then show me and I will see. Command me and I will obey. Lead me and I will follow. If my feeble life can be used by You, I give it. I am Yours, my King and my Prince."

Twitch bowed his head. He had never dared speak such words before, for he knew such an oath demanded pursuit, but this moment and place had caused his heart to spill out. It felt good…and a little strange. Twitch shuddered with the sense that a curtain had been drawn open behind him…a curtain hiding another world.

Overwhelmed by the thought, Twitch ducked his head and glanced to the right—just in time to see Sir Baylor lunge straight at him with shoulder lowered.

Twitch tried to stand, but Baylor hit him square in the chest, and they careened to the ground, rolling perilously close to the ridge that fell off far below the clearing. Twitch gasped, his lungs collapsing from the force of the blow, as Baylor scrambled to his feet and drew his sword.

Twitch reached for his chest with his left hand and his sword with his right. His response seemed like slow motion compared to Baylor's. His confusion mounted as Baylor turned his back to him. The mighty knight assumed a two-handed hanging guard stance, facing something Twitch had only imagined in his nightmares.

Just beyond Baylor stood a massive dark warrior, who growled and cursed as he recovered his sword from a vertical cut that had split the ground where Twitch had just been kneeling. The warrior unleashed a volley of cuts and slices toward Baylor. Their swords collided in brilliant, ear-piercing clashes.

Twitch instinctively backed away on his elbows, still trying desperately to regain his air. The grip on his lungs finally released, and he drew a shaky breath.

Twitch rose up to one knee as he saw Baylor catch a slice with his sword and quickly counter with one of his own that caught the dark warrior off guard. The warrior cursed and stepped back, and Baylor capitalized on this slight advantage. He feigned a thrust but then quickly changed to a powerful two-handed slice that blasted into his enemy's shoulder. Thrown off balance, the warrior stumbled toward the ridge. Baylor advanced with a thrust, and the warrior lost his footing. He screamed and grasped for the edge of the ridge as he tumbled over. Baylor then turned to engage another massive warrior who had come at him from behind.

"Move, kid!" Twitch heard a different voice scream from his right. He turned just in time to glimpse another grisly blade arcing toward him.

Twitch's stomach rose to his throat. He dove forward, away from the deadly cut, and felt the tip of the blade slice through the back of his tunic, grazing his right shoulder. He hit the ground and rolled to his back again.

What is happening? he wondered, fear filling his heart as yet another dark warrior loomed over him. There was nothing Twitch could do to stop the inevitable. He closed his eyes and turned his head away as the glinting steel thundered down like a lightning bolt.

This time, the clang of metal on metal was so close to his head it hurt his ears. The scuffle of boots cast dirt and pine needles into his face. He looked up to see a knight maneuvering his sword so deftly that Twitch could hardly follow it. Slowly the warrior retreated as the knight advanced. Twitch once again crawled away from the fray and quickly regained his feet.

The clearing now vibrated with the intensity of battle. Two other knights had appeared from the woods to join Sir Baylor and his comrade. Each knight was engaged in a life-or-death duel with an evil warrior who seemed to defy Twitch's perception of reality. The knights' clothing was subdued, but each clearly bore the mark of the Prince. They seemed fearless. Each fought for his life and yet for something more.

These men fought not as individuals, but as a finely honed team. When one knight faltered, another deftly moved to protect his companion, then quickly reengaged his foe again. As a force of four, the knights formed an impenetrable wall of protection. Twitch finally drew his sword as well, but it seemed a paltry action when he realized just how inadequate his skills were in comparison.

"Kessler, Drake's flank!" Twitch heard Sir Baylor command as he wounded an opponent, then ran to assist another knight. The one named Kessler moved with the speed of a panther to engage the warrior attacking the knight who had saved Twitch. After a few more moments of tenacious fighting, the dark warriors disengaged and retreated into the surrounding trees.

"Where did they come from?" the knight named Kessler asked as he and his comrades scanned the area for more threats. Sweat dripped from ringlets of black hair that hung around his handsome, dark-skinned face. He was the first to sheath his sword.

Sir Baylor just shook his head. With narrow eyes he continued his scan.

"Yes, what happened, Commander?" The one called Drake turned to face Baylor. He was a large knight, nearly equal in size to the warriors they had just faced. His sandy hair and bright blue eyes did little to diminish the fierceness of his countenance. "You know as well as we that they don't attack without a purpose."

"You're right, and I didn't expect them here." Baylor sheathed his sword and turned to face Twitch for the first time. "Where's Gustav?"

Twitch was still stunned by what he'd just experienced. He shook his head as if to awaken from a bad dream. "He didn't come, sir."

The fourth knight abandoned his search at the perimeter of the clearing and walked toward the rest of the group, his sword and long knife still firmly in his grip. He walked past Twitch as if he wasn't there and stood before Baylor.

"We delayed another day for nothing? And risked this exposure?" he asked Baylor. The intensity of battle still lingered in his brown eyes. A half-grown mustache and sparse goatee gave his youthful face a roguish appearance.

"Easy, Purcell," Baylor said. "We lost nothing."

"And gained nothing," Drake added.

Kessler grinned. "You blokes needed to sharpen up a bit anyway." He slapped Purcell on the shoulder as he walked to the ridge leading down from the mountain. "What's next, Commander?"

Purcell sneered briefly at Kessler, then sighed and sheathed his sword. He spun his long knife about his palm before snapping it into its own sheath. "Shall we prepare to leave, sir?"

"It appears so." Baylor shot a quick glance toward Twitch. "Rendezvous at the river. I'll be there to join you shortly."

The three knights saluted and began their descent down Mount Resolute. Baylor stared hard at Twitch, who was keenly aware that his cheek was convulsing again.

Baylor crossed his arms across his chest. "Why didn't Gustav come with you…and why are you here?"

"I…I wanted to talk to you about—sir, what just happened?" Twitch rubbed his chest, wondering if he found it difficult to breathe because of what he'd just seen or because of Baylor's impact on him.

"That was just a glimpse of the war I warned Gustav about." Baylor looked from one side of the clearing to the other, then settled his eyes back on Twitch. "Why they attacked you is peculiar. Perhaps they thought you were Gustav."

"I don't understand," Twitch said.

"You don't have to." Baylor walked to the edge of the ridge. "You'd best follow me down and be on your way."

Twitch stayed close to Baylor. The first part of the descent was steep, but the grade became gradual enough for Twitch to walk beside Sir Baylor.

"Who were those warriors?" he finally mustered the courage to ask.

Baylor seemed to ignore the question, and Twitch didn't dare ask twice. Somehow he felt guilty about the recent skirmish, as if it were somehow his fault.

They walked a few more paces.

"They were Shadow Warriors under the command of Lucius." Baylor said it matter-of-factly, but chills ran up Twitch's spine.

They came to another lesser ridge that led to their final descent. Baylor hesitated, briefly peering into the gathering dusk.

"Who are those knights who fought with you?" Twitch asked. "Who are you...really?"

Baylor looked over at Twitch.

"Look, son. You've already seen too much, and you shouldn't even be here. These men—they are the tip of the Prince's sword. Their commitment is total, their sacrifice is great, and their skills are unmatched. I've searched the kingdom over to find them. They put their lives on the line for the King and His Son every day, and sometimes..." Baylor turned away. When he turned back, his jaw was clenched and his eyes red. "Sometimes they fall. What I ask from them—what the Prince asks of them—is much, and I would give my life to protect them. Their secrecy is part of that protection."

Twitch swallowed hard. Something stirred deep within him, something he had never felt before. For one brief moment of his life he had been witness to a whole new world of conflict and purpose. It was a glimpse he couldn't forget. It also told him that Sir Baylor was every-thing he seemed to be and more.

"I want to join you, sir." Twitch could not stop the words if he'd tried. They had formed deep in his soul and spilled out before he could think them away. It was a defining moment, a moment that might thrust him into a whole new world about which he knew nothing—a world of battle!

Baylor halted and stared at Twitch; then a slight smile crossed his lips. His gaze softened as he put a hand on Twitch's shoulder.

"Don't take this wrong, son, but this unit isn't something you join. My knights are carefully selected, and Gustav—"

Baylor froze, and his eyes regained their steely gaze. He grabbed Twitch's tunic and shoved him up next to a tree. He held his finger to his lips, then quietly drew his sword. Twitch's heart began to race again. Were the Shadow Warriors back? Were there more this time?

Baylor readied his sword. He turned away from Twitch, his muscles taut and ready to fight. Twitch saw him reach for a chain around his neck and lift a small silver disk out of his tunic. He turned away and brought his hand to his face, then replaced the disk inside his shirt.

"Stay here," Baylor whispered over his shoulder.

Twitch watched as the man stealthily made his way through the trees along the ridge. His face began convulsing again. He drew his own sword and tried to see through the shadows of the retreating day. In another moment, Baylor had disappeared completely, and Twitch strug-gled to keep his fear in check.

Something shuffled behind him, and he spun about with his sword, fully expecting another grisly weapon to be descending on him. A squir-rel raced across the forest floor and scurried up a tree. Twitch exhaled with relief. The faint sound of deep voices filtered through the foliage, but the words were unintelligible. Finally Baylor appeared again, his sword sheathed. Twitch quickly sheathed his own and waited.

Baylor walked directly to Twitch and put his fists on his hips. He eyed him up and down with a perplexed look on his face. It was an awk-ward moment, and Twitch's cheek seemed worse than ever.

"What's your name?" Baylor asked bluntly.

"Twitch, sir."

Annoyance flashed across Baylor's face. "What's your real name?"

Twitch studied the ground. He couldn't remember the last time someone had asked him for his real name. He looked back up at the stern face of Sir Baylor.

"My name is Quinlan."

SIX

LEAST OF THE LEAST

Baylor motioned toward the ridge.

"Come, Sir Quinlan. You're riding with us."

Baylor immediately stepped over the ridge and on toward the base of Mount Resolute. Quinlan stood still, stunned by Sir Baylor's apparent change of mind. He had fully expected his request to be denied, for his skills as a knight were nothing compared to Tav's, not to mention the knights who rode with Sir Baylor. Quinlan knew he could spend his whole life in training and still not achieve what he had just seen.

He ran to catch up to Sir Baylor. "I should tell Tav and his parents. They are my only family and will want to know."

"We need to leave immediately." Baylor's words felt cold, and his demeanor toward Quinlan seemed to harden. "However, we can afford to give you a few minutes to gather your things and say good-bye."

Quinlan didn't say another word. He knew Baylor's offer to join him would only happen once, and he didn't want to jeopardize that in any way. Yet second thoughts began even before he had mounted Kobalt. Quinlan had come to Mount Resolute looking for answers to a few questions, not seeking to abandon everything in his life in a moment. Yet here he was, following a man he knew almost nothing about into a completely unknown future. The only thing he really knew was that he was ill-equipped and unprepared—the least of the least—for whatever lay ahead.

When they arrived at Quinlan's home, Baylor waited outside. Tav was still away with Mirya. After explaining the scratches on his face and hands to Tav's parents, Quinlan told them what he'd decided to do. Tav's father looked sternly at him, then went outside to speak with Baylor. Tav's mother put her hand on Quinlan's arm. "Are you sure about this, Twitch?"

Quinlan nodded at the woman who had been his substitute mother for the past nine years. "Yes, I'm sure." He put his hand on hers. "Thank you for all you've done for me. Someday I hope to be able to repay you."

She squeezed his arm. "Sons don't repay a father or a mother for raising them."

Quinlan lowered his head, moved by her words. He looked into her worried face and quickly hugged her, then headed for his room to gather a few belongings.

He was nearly ready when Tav burst into his room. "What crazy nonsense is this?"

Quinlan finished tying up his knapsack and turned to face his friend.

"What happened to you?" Tav took a few steps closer to inspect the scratches across Quinlan's face.

Quinlan realized that Disty was glaring at him from Tav's shoulder and baring its teeth. He pointed at the paytha, which growled. "Tav, you need to get rid of that thing!"

"What are you talking about?" Tav reached up to pet Disty, who settled a bit.

Quinlan held up his hands to show Tav the bite marks. "Bli attacked me for no reason. It just went mad."

Tav looked confused. He walked over to a table and tapped on it. Disty scurried down his arm onto the table and chortled softly while Tav stroked its neck.

"That probably had something to do with Baylor too," he said. "What's going on, chum?"

"Sir Baylor said I could go with him, Tav." Quinlan hesitated. "And I'm going."

"You can't do this." Tav lowered his voice. "Baylor is crazy! There's no telling what will happen to you."

"He's not crazy, Tav. You and I both know that. Tonight I saw something…" Quinlan looked at the ground and slowly shook his head. He looked up and took a step toward his friend. "You should come with me!"

Disty growled again, and Quinlan backed away.

"Whoa, Disty—what's wrong with you tonight?" Tav said. The critter scurried closer to him and begged to be lifted back onto Tav's shoulder. Tav obliged.

"You are what Sir Baylor needs, much more so than I." Quinlan imagined both of them on a quest of great purpose for the Prince, just as they had dreamed of years ago. "We could do this together."

"Leave my father without any help at all? Leave Mirya? I don't think so, chum." Tav looked deep into Quinlan's eyes, then forced a weak smile. "This isn't for me. It's for you."

He held out his arm, and Quinlan grabbed it.

"You be careful," Tav said. "Whether Baylor's crazy or not, you be careful."

Quinlan nodded, then walked outside, where Tav's father was exchanging heated words with Sir Baylor. He hushed when Quinlan appeared. Quinlan's farewell to Tav's father was wordless in keeping with their reserved relationship, but he still rode away with a lump in his throat.

Quinlan trailed closely behind Sir Baylor until they reached the little grove near the river where Sir Drake, Sir Kessler, and Sir Purcell were waiting. "Gentlemen," Baylor announced as he dismounted, "this is Sir Quinlan, the newest member of our unit."

The look of consternation on the faces of the knights made Quinlan cringe, which set his cheek to twitching.

"You're kidding," Purcell said. "What's going on, Commander?"

Baylor crossed his arms. "Quinlan is our fifth knight. We will train him as such."

"Commander"—Drake motioned with his head—"can we have a word with you?"

Baylor clenched his jaw and walked a few paces away with the three knights. Their conversation was hushed and unintelligible to Quinlan at first, but soon the volume of the voices rose.

"Commander, our lives depend on each other's skills." Drake's deep voice carried to Quinlan's ears. "This lad can hardly handle a sword, let alone handle himself in a fight."

"That's right," Purcell joined in. "He's no replacement for Sir Freyton and certainly not his equal. One or all of us could get killed because of his inexperience. You must reconsider!"

That Kessler remained silent was small compensation for the humiliation Quinlan felt. He walked to the far side of Kobalt, intending to ride back to Burkfield and forget this day had ever happened. He checked the girth and set his foot into the stirrup.

"Do you two have anything else you want to say?" Quinlan heard Baylor ask sternly.

Silence was the only reply.

"Then mount up. We ride for Arimil—all of us. We only have a few hours of moonlight."

Quinlan hesitated with his foot in the stirrup. He completely agreed with Purcell and Drake. He could never truly be a replacement for any of them, and he was just as confused as they were about why Baylor had chosen him.

He slowly lifted himself onto Kobalt as the other knights recovered their steeds. He felt trapped. Nothing he could do would feel right now. He watched with great trepidation as Baylor led the knights toward the road that led to Arimil. Quinlan delayed until he was last in line, but he followed.

Not long after they began, Kessler broke from Purcell and Drake and joined Quinlan at the rear. "Is Burkfield home for you?" he asked.

"For as long as I can remember," Quinlan replied.

"So you've got family there?"

"Not really," Quinlan said. "Tav's—Gustav's—family took me in when I was just a lad, after my parents died. They're as close as I have to family."

Kessler nodded. He leaned over to Quinlan and spoke more softly than usual. "Don't let Drake and Purcell rattle you. They're good men once you get to know them."

Quinlan glanced at Kessler and caught a quick wink accompanied by a crooked grin. He forced a smile in return, grateful for Kessler's attempt to make him feel better. The overture couldn't change reality, though. Everyone in the unit knew Quinlan shouldn't be there—everyone, apparently, except Baylor.

They had not ridden far before the moon set and the roadway grew too dark for the horses to navigate. Baylor chose a secluded grove of trees for their camp. The following morning they were on their way by daybreak.

At midafternoon, they arrived in the little town of Briar Grove, where Baylor purchased provisions for the unit and a few items for Quinlan. Now fully outfitted, they resumed their journey to Arimil.

"You ride with me, Quinlan," Baylor commanded.

Quinlan cantered Kobalt up next to Baylor.

"There are three rules in this unit that are never broken."

Baylor squinted meaningfully at Quinlan as if trying to convince himself he had made the right choice. Quinlan waited for the commander to continue.

Baylor held up one finger.

"We live and die by the Articles of the Code and by the Sword of the Prince. Learn and live them well."

Baylor held up a second finger.

"Secrecy is our life. As far as the rest of the kingdom is concerned, you do not exist."

A third finger went up.

"My word is final—always! Do you understand?"

Quinlan nodded.

"Very well." Baylor nodded. "I'm sure you have questions. I can answer some of them now. Others will be answered for you as your training progresses." He looked at Quinlan as if he were waiting.

There were a hundred questions Quinlan wanted to ask, but there was only one he absolutely had to know the answer to. "Why did you allow me to join the unit?"

Baylor stared blankly at Quinlan for a long while; then his gaze went back to the road. Finally he turned and looked straight into Quinlan's eyes. "Tell me why you were kneeling on Mount Resolute."

Quinlan looked away, reliving that powerful moment in his mind. Emotions flooded his bosom as he remembered his words.

"I made an oath to the Prince," he said, "to live my life completely for Him and give Him all that I have." Quinlan looked down at Kobalt's mane. "But I don't have much to offer Him." He looked back at Baylor. His cheek twitched, and he shrugged.

Baylor's gaze went deep. Quinlan wondered if the man had forgotten his question, but he dared not ask it again.

When Baylor finally spoke, his voice was hushed. "When you made your oath to the Prince, you stepped through the veil of deception and began to see the kingdom as it really is. It is this reality we live and fight in every day." He gestured to the other men. "Those knights who are truly dedicated to the Prince see the true kingdom well, but those who are not—and there are many—do not see it at all."

"The true kingdom—is that what I saw yesterday?"

"Yes, partly."

Quinlan knit his brow. "It's darker than I want it to be."

"And brighter than you know," Baylor replied. "When the veil is gone, you see everything much more clearly, both the dark and the light. You only saw the dark yesterday, but the light is so much greater!"

Quinlan nodded, accepting that. "What is this unit's mission in serving the Prince, sir?"

Baylor looked away to the horizon. "The highest mission of all is to carry the truth of the Prince into the far regions of the kingdom.

Though we look for opportunities to do that, there are men and women greater than we who accomplish this mission with courage and skill." Baylor turned again to Quinlan. "We support those men and women… often without their even knowing it."

Quinlan could not help the smile that crossed his lips. In spite of all of his inadequacies, in spite of all of his awkwardness, he knew he was created for this purpose too.

"How, Commander?" he asked. "How do you support them?"

"After the Son of the King gave His great commission to the Knights of the Prince in Chessington, our missions began to spread across the kingdom in all directions, but Lucius and his minions opposed us every step of the way." Baylor's eyes became fierce. "My knights and I support those who carry the truth of the Prince by protecting them from Lucius's evil plots. Our swords protect and deliver the truth that sets people free. We fight against Lucius and his Shadow Warriors for the sake of those who believe *and* for those who do not."

Baylor looked away and took a deep breath. "In this kingdom there is little glory in standing between the knights on mission for the Prince and the evil that wants to devour them. What you will sacrifice, Quinlan, may never be known this side of the Great Sea, yet our missions have the potential to change the course of the kingdom."

Quinlan pondered Baylor's words. They inspired him and saddened him at the same time.

"This reality I speak of is potentially frightful, and our missions require much from the men in my unit, who are knights of great courage and skill." Baylor paused and looked once more at Quinlan. "You can still turn back. There are many other ways to serve the Prince other than becoming one of the Swords of Valor."

Quinlan hesitated, thinking hard. And somehow, deep within, he found a strength he didn't know was there. He had never experienced anything quite like it before. In one day he already felt changed, and he wondered what a lifetime of such service would do.

"I cannot choose to ignore the truth, nor can I have peace when that truth requires me to respond. No, Commander, I will not turn back. I have little to offer the Prince and even less to offer you, but if you will have me, I will serve."

It was nearly imperceptible, but the right side of Baylor's lips lifted slightly.

"There's more to you than most people think, young Quinlan."

Quinlan shook his head. "Tav told me that once before too, but I doubt—"

"Gustav? Really?"

"Yes sir." Quinlan thought a little sadly of the friend who had been as close as a brother for most of his life. "You remind me of him, sir."

They were silent for a time.

"My place here belongs to Tav," Quinlan finally said. "He deserves it more than I."

"Everyone must choose for himself," Baylor said.

"He's been a good brother to me."

Baylor just nodded and said no more.

That evening they made an early camp, and Baylor began to train Quinlan. Their swords reverberated through the woods, and Quinlan gave his all, but he struggled. By nightfall, he was exhausted, and he could tell Baylor was frustrated.

Drake and Purcell would have almost nothing to do with him. Kessler seemed his only friend. The man's cheerful spirit eased Quinlan's feelings of complete inadequacy, and Quinlan rather enjoyed Kessler's lighthearted jabs at the other knights. Quinlan wondered if perhaps this was Kessler's way of defending him in the unit. Whatever the reason, Quinlan was grateful for one kind face.

For a late meal, Quinlan speared a slab of venison and some bread, then went to sit beside Kessler. Baylor and Drake were already asleep, and Purcell was off sharpening his knives while taking the first watch.

"Why are we going to Arimil?" Quinlan asked.

"We won't know till we get there," Kessler replied.

"I don't understand," Quinlan said. "How can we have a mission in a city that is nearly a three days' ride from Burkfield and not know why we are going there? How does the commander decide on the mission?"

"The commander doesn't decide the mission," Kessler said. "It comes from Taras."

Quinlan scratched his head. "Who's Taras?"

Kessler hesitated. "He's a Silent Warrior. He only speaks to Sir Baylor."

Quinlan looked at Kessler to see if he was joking. He wasn't. "Have you seen Taras?" Quinlan asked.

"No. None of us have."

Quinlan took a bite of bread as he thought about Kessler's answer. "You must really—"

"Trust him? Yes, we do." Kessler plucked a blade of long grass and began to chew the end of it. "We get some crazy missions, but his information is always spot-on. Yes, we all trust him with our lives."

Kessler leaned closer to Quinlan. "You want to know what's really amazing? The commander can spot a Shadow Warrior a hundred paces away. We've all gotten pretty good at it, but not from that distance and not with his consistency. He's saved our necks many times by putting his own life on the line. He's a great man, and you're fortunate to be serving under him."

Quinlan swallowed his last bite, glad the darkness hid the twitching muscle in his face. "I don't want to disappoint him…or the others. I just don't know if I've got what it takes."

Kessler smiled and put a hand on Quinlan's shoulder. "You wouldn't be here if the commander didn't think you have what it takes. I think you need to start trusting him too."

Quinlan shot Kessler a weak grin. "Thanks."

Kessler nodded, then went to his bedroll. Quinlan soon found his own and settled in for a night's sleep. He drifted into slumber, both dreading and anticipating what awaited them in Arimil.

SEVEN

WORTHINGTON

Two more days of travel brought Baylor and his men to the outskirts of Arimil, on Arrethtrae's western shore. It was beautiful, lush country, and the salty smell of the sea was a new sensation for Quinlan. Baylor led them to a hill overlooking the eastern road that entered the city. Careful to stay out of sight, they watched the road until a small detachment of five knights appeared, traveling from the east.

"There's our man, gentlemen." Baylor pointed toward the front of the detachment. "The one in blue."

Quinlan had assumed this noble-looking knight was the leader, but the one riding next to him also caught his eye. She rode her steed with confidence, and even from this distance, he could tell she was a very attractive young woman.

The other knights, though, seemed focused only on the man Baylor had pointed out. "Who is he, sir?" Drake asked.

"That's Sir Worthington of Thecia, the one we've come to protect," Baylor said. "Taras tells me he's a prime target for Lucius, and it's our job to make sure he stays alive."

"Why is he a target?" Purcell asked.

"Evidently he has great potential to bring many to the Prince," Baylor said. "Both the Silent Warriors and the Shadow Warriors have become quite adept at discerning who is going to significantly affect the kingdom, often even before the person himself knows it. Such is the case with Worthington."

Quinlan was still adjusting to this new world of warfare. "Do you think he knows?"

Baylor looked at him as if he were waiting for the rest of the question.

"About the war, I mean—and that he's a part of it?"

Baylor looked back at Worthington. "A man like that knows. He just doesn't realize how close he is to it—not yet, anyway. Knights of the Prince don't usually know what's happening until they are under full attack. By then it's a retreat-and-defend scenario. We're going to do our best to keep that from happening here."

By now the detachment had passed on and entered the city. Baylor turned and addressed his knights.

"The information I have predicts an attack on Worthington here in Arimil. Whether it is simply a disruptive attack to nullify his work in the city or an all-out assassination attempt is unknown. We must be prepared for anything."

Quinlan watched the other knights as Baylor briefed them. They wore the faces of men called to battle, and he admired their sense of commitment and duty.

"Worthington and his men will be conducting recruitment meetings and specialized training in the haven for the next two days," Baylor told them. "We have until sundown to learn all we can about this haven, the city, the surrounding area, and Worthington and his knights. We'll be doing three-stage protection. Drake, you and I will cover outer perimeter and entry routes to the city. Kessler, you have central perimeter, and Purcell, you'll be on the inside. I need you as close to Worthington as possible. You know what to do."

"Yes, Commander," Purcell said with a wink and a grin.

"Quinlan, you do reconnaissance with Kessler for now," Baylor continued. "We meet back here at sundown. That will give us enough time to report and get positioned before nightfall. Questions?"

Quinlan had a hundred but dared not ask one.

"Do your jobs well, men, so that tomorrow we aren't surprised."

The knights saluted and separated. Quinlan rode with Kessler and Purcell toward the city while Drake and Baylor headed southeast to investigate the southern perimeter. Once inside the city, Purcell split from Kessler and Quinlan.

"How many Shadow Warriors will we face?" Quinlan asked Kessler as they rode down a city street.

"Most attacks are by two or three Shadow Warriors, and that is plenty. The Swords of Valor augment the Silent Warriors and take missions of protection that may or may not event out."

"Event out?"

"Every time we are called, the mission is real, but not every mission ends in a fight. When swords cross, we call that an event."

Quinlan nodded. "I see."

"We are given missions when the predicted warrior count is five or less. Anything more than that, the Silent Warriors are involved—and they may be anyway, depending on the importance of the mission. We can never tell. Sometimes the most innocuous missions end up becoming critical events. It also depends on which Shadow Warriors are identified as incoming threats."

Kessler looked over at Quinlan with as serious a look as he had yet seen on the man. "There are some Shadow Warriors you just don't ever want to face."

Quinlan swallowed hard as Kessler continued. "Five warriors or less is a skirmish. Fifteen or less, a fray. Fifty, a conflict. More than that is a battle."

"How about a war?"

Kessler smiled. "That's what we're in right now, my friend, and it's all around us."

"Of course," Quinlan said with a sheepish grin. "The commander mentioned three-stage protection. What is it?"

"Stage one is outer-perimeter protection. Baylor identifies the size and direction of the approaching Shadow Warrior force. With early detection, Baylor has often been able to thwart an attack before it starts, especially if it's a single warrior. Stage two is inner-perimeter protection,

the primary and preferred fight zone for anything greater than four warriors. Stage three is protection right next to the target. If the fight gets
that close, we haven't done our job and things are getting desperate.
Depending on the situation, target extraction is a possibility. That's part
of Purcell's reconnaissance—to determine a safe extraction route. By
then our cover is blown and all bets are off."

Quinlan shook his head, again feeling completely out of his league.
It would take a decade of training before he could contribute anything
to the unit…if he didn't get killed first. He imagined Tav in his place—
clearly the wiser choice—but thinking that way brought instant discouragement, so he forced himself to concentrate on the mission at
hand.

Quinlan spent the next three hours learning as much as possible
from Kessler—asking questions when necessary while trying not to be a
hindrance to their work. He was extremely grateful for being assigned
with him and knew that Baylor had matched them for more than just
mission fulfillment.

At sundown the five men met once again on the knoll overlooking
the city. Baylor reached down with a stick and drew a rough outline of
Arimil and the coastline in the dirt. "Purcell, you first," he commanded.

"The haven meets on the stable grounds on the southeastern edge
of the city. Worthington and his team sleep in tents nearby." Purcell
pointed to the location of the haven and the tents on the ground map.

Baylor looked disappointed.

"That's tougher to defend," Kessler whispered to Quinlan. "Get
ready for double night watches."

"There are four other Knights of the Prince on Worthington's
team," Purcell continued. "Three look like they can handle themselves
well. Worthington himself is solid. The haven is small and ill-prepared
for anything significant. Other than their leader, Sir Borden, I wouldn't
count on any of their swords in a fray. The training and meetings begin
after the morning meal and finish just before sundown. Near as I can
tell, they're expecting forty to fifty attendees. I should be able to stay
close to Worthington all day."

"Good," Baylor replied. "Coordinate with Kessler on communication signals and possible extraction routes. Kessler, what did you find?"

"There's a seven-foot stone wall here"—he drew it on the ground map—"that will offer some protection on the northern and eastern sides of the location, although there are trees and some fencing that could also provide cover for an attacker." He added more detail to the map as he talked. "A wooden fence borders the southeast. There are numerous shops inside the city to the west with the main thoroughfare two streets away. If warriors make it into the city undetected, they've got multiple access points to the stables—tough to cover with just two men."

"If my information is correct, they shouldn't be in the city yet," Baylor replied. "Unless they're seafarers, but Taras assured me they had that covered. Anything else?"

Kessler shook his head. "If an event happens in the city, things could get messy."

Baylor nodded. "In that case, Drake, you're with Kessler guarding the city side of the haven. There's moderate cover in the surrounding country, so I should be able to spot warriors readily if they approach from the east. The key to success for this mission will be communication. Quinlan, that's where you come in. I want you positioned out of sight of the attendees, north of the stone wall." He pointed to the spot on the map. "That will allow you to see my signals as to warrior force size and direction. Do you have the flag and hand signals down?"

Quinlan nodded.

"Good. You need to patrol the outside of that stone wall and also be able to see Kessler or Drake in case the attack comes from the city. You will relay information either direction, depending on what happens. Is that clear?"

"Yes, Commander." Quinlan tried to sound confident.

"Very well." Baylor wiped the ground map clean and stood up. "At night we'll collapse to a close perimeter around Worthington's tents. Purcell, Quinlan, you have the first watch—then Drake and Kessler. I'll take the third watch."

Baylor gathered his men in a circle, then drew his sword. "Remember who you serve, Knights of the Prince."

The other men drew their swords and brought them together in the center of their circle.

"Swords of Valor for Him," the men said in unison.

The Swords of Valor were in position before breakfast the next day. Quinlan settled into his place just on the north side of the stone wall, near a spot where the stones had partially fallen. He could see Baylor on a knoll east of the haven and would easily be able to relay any flag signals the commander gave. He could also see Kessler across the outer yard and one street into the city. Kessler was dressed as a commoner, browsing shops. Drake was nearby but not visible to Quinlan.

The hours wore on. Quinlan struggled to keep his attention keen, reminding himself that Shadow Warriors could arrive at any moment. The clang of swords wielded by knights and trainees just inside the wall helped with the boredom. In the afternoon, Quinlan heard the distant sure voice of a young man teaching others, though the words were too faint for Quinlan to discern any content. He assumed the voice belonged to Worthington.

Later, Quinlan heard a different voice much closer—just on the other side of the wall, in fact. It was a female voice with an unusual accent that enticed him to listen closely to every word. "The sword is the embodiment of the Code, our primary weapon to defend the weak and protect the innocent. It is our greatest defense against the forces of evil."

The voice was confident and yet lovely. Quinlan was grateful he couldn't see the speaker, for he imagined she would be as charming as she sounded, and that would send him into his typical awkward state. Still, hearing her instruct trainees for the rest of the afternoon provided a delightful distraction from Quinlan's tedious lookout duties.

The day ended as uneventfully as it had started, much to Quinlan's relief. After Purcell shared more information he had gathered about the haven and Worthington himself, the valor knights retreated to their night watches.

The next day passed much as the previous one had. By late afternoon, the meetings were wrapping up. Quinlan looked toward Baylor—all clear. Then he looked toward Kessler and passed on the signal. He could hear the final bout of sword training just over the wall and wondered how many trainees were taking the exercises seriously.

"Been standing here long?"

Quinlan jumped at the voice behind him. He reached for his sword as he turned.

"Whoa, sir. I'm a friend." The man offered his hand. "Worthington of Berwick, in Cameria."

Quinlan relaxed and grasped the man's hand. "It's an honor, sir."

Worthington tilted his head slightly, then smiled. Wavy brown hair flowed back from a handsome face, and his weary gray eyes held a down-to-earth friendliness. If he was supposed to be someone great, he didn't seem to know it.

"Are you from Arimil?" The man spoke with the same intriguing accent as the young female knight. Quinlan suspected they were both from the same region—perhaps husband and wife.

"No, I'm not from here." Quinlan wondered how important it was to keep his identity a secret from Worthington. They were both Knights of the Prince, after all, fighting for the same cause.

"So what are you doing here?" Worthington asked.

At that instant, over Worthington's shoulder, Quinlan spotted Baylor's signal—three Shadow Warriors approaching from the north! His heart began to race. He glanced north but saw nothing; then he turned and saw Kessler drawing his sword. Kessler signaled that two warriors were approaching from the south, then disappeared before Quinlan could pass Baylor's message on.

Five Shadow Warriors! Quinlan wasn't sure what to do. Where was Purcell?

"You seem concerned," Worthington said. "Is there something I can help you—"

Quinlan drew his sword and Worthington backed away, his hand to the hilt of his own weapon. "What's the meaning of this?" he asked sternly.

"Sir Worthington, I am a fellow Knight of the Prince," Quinlan said quickly. "Shadow Warriors are coming this way. We need to get you back into the haven."

At first Worthington looked as if he thought Quinlan was crazy. Then his eyes opened wide, and he drew his sword. "Watch out!" he screamed.

Quinlan turned just in time to see a Shadow Warrior lunging toward them from behind a group of trees. Another warrior was behind him, closing in quickly. The closest warrior slammed his sword into Quinlan's and sent him stumbling to the side, then immediately attacked Worthington, the obvious target.

Quinlan recovered to one knee and prepared to face the second charging warrior, hoping that Worthington could hold his own until Baylor arrived. Just then, he saw Purcell leap through the broken-down section of the stone wall to face the second warrior. His knife was drawn before his feet hit the ground.

Quinlan turned to help Worthington, who appeared to be in dire trouble. The young knight watched in horror as the first warrior finished a crosscut, followed by a thrust toward Worthington's heart. But then Quinlan caught a glimpse of steel pass just above his right shoulder. Purcell's perfectly thrown knife sank into the Shadow Warrior's side, causing him to pull back on his deadly thrust.

The warrior screamed and turned on Quinlan in fury. Fear washed over Quinlan as he readied himself to face his first real enemy.

He caught a vertical cut and tried to counter, but the warrior quickly blocked it and advanced with another slice. Just then Quinlan heard Worthington shout behind him and engage with what Quinlan realized had to be the third warrior Baylor had seen. The clash of steel from the three fights meshed with the sound of training just on the other side of the haven wall.

In spite of his wound, the warrior Quinlan was facing made cuts and slices so powerful that Quinlan found himself in constant retreat. After two more advances, however, the injured warrior began to falter, and Quinlan risked an advance. The warrior deflected two of his cuts, then backed away, stumbled, and disappeared into the trees.

Thankful that the fight was over and that he had survived it, Quinlan turned to help Worthington. But Worthington's opponent had maneuvered him away from Quinlan and Purcell, toward the end of the stone wall, and looked to be one slice shy of overpowering the man. Quinlan started toward them, knowing there was no way he could reach them in time. Just then Sir Baylor appeared on horseback from around the end of the wall and charged the warrior, bringing him off of Worthington. Behind him appeared the young female knight, sword drawn and ready.

Relieved, Quinlan turned back to help Purcell. Once Purcell's Shadow Warrior saw another knight coming, he too backed out of the fight and disappeared into the trees.

"Kessler signaled two more in the city," Quinlan said.

"Come." Purcell took off in that direction. Quinlan followed, looking over his shoulder to see that the warrior attacking Worthington had abandoned his fight as well. The young woman stared in Quinlan's direction as other knights from Worthington's unit began appearing from behind the wall. Worthington would be well protected now.

Quinlan and Purcell ran to the street where Kessler had last been seen.

"He went south," Quinlan reported.

They ran past three shops and then saw both Drake and Kessler walking toward them from an alleyway. Bright red blood spilled from a cut on Drake's arm. He didn't seem to notice it.

"They attacked from the south," Kessler said, "but we were able to hold them off—quite easily, for some reason."

"It was a diversion," Purcell said. "Three more attacked from the north at the same time."

Kessler's eyes widened. "Worthington?"

"Safe," Purcell replied. "But it was close—a third-stage event. Baylor showed up at the last moment."

Drake shook his head. "Five warriors, split attack, single target—that's a first."

The four men stood in silence for a moment.

"They're on to us," Purcell said gravely, "and adjusting."

"Yes, feels a bit like a game of chess with high stakes, doesn't it?" Kessler said, then smiled broadly. "Are we knights or are we pawns, gentlemen?"

"Must you be so cheerful about everything?" Purcell grumbled, turning back toward the haven. Drake and Kessler laughed and followed behind. Quinlan joined them, but not in the laughter, for he was feeling quite like a pawn. 🔲

EIGHT

A NEW KIND OF ENEMY

 After Arimil, Quinlan continued his training each night with Sir Baylor. He was slowly improving, but it was not enough—at least not enough for Purcell and Drake to think him a worthy member of the unit.

Quinlan had to agree with them. He still felt like a child among men.

The next mission for the Swords of Valor began four weeks later. They arrived near the northern haven of Garriston early in the morning. According to Kessler, they had been there numerous times before and had thus far been able to spoil all attempts by the Shadow Warriors to destroy or seriously disrupt the haven. Missions to Garriston had almost become routine, though Baylor cautioned the knights to be vigilant just the same. His ability to identify the warriors early should still provide significant advantage, but their experience at Arimil had indicated the Shadow Warriors were adopting new tactics.

The Swords of Valor gathered in a circle while Baylor briefed them on what was to happen and what to do if events went awry. Then he drew his sword and held it before him. The other knights did the same.

"Remember who you serve, Knights of the Prince."

The five swords came together in the center of their circle.

"Swords of Valor for Him!" the men voiced in unity. Then they sheathed their swords, mounted up, and headed for their lookouts.

Soon the men were positioned in a semicircle around the haven, all within view of the commander. Quinlan was stationed nearest Baylor. As instructed, he tethered Kobalt to a tree a short distance away so as not to give his lookout position away.

Quinlan heard music in the distance. In an effort to reach more people in the surrounding region, the haven was hosting a festival. Quinlan wished he could partake of the festivities, but Baylor had insisted that their presence remain a secret. Only in the Kingdom Across the Sea would many of the men and women of the haven know what was accomplished for them by the valor knights.

Baylor had predicted that four Shadow Warriors would attack from the southeast, which meant that Kessler and Drake would face them first. They would have to hold them off until Baylor confirmed that his tactical information was correct, for he couldn't take a chance and let warriors slip through from another direction.

"Stay sharp and alert, men," the commander had ordered. "No mission against Lucius is routine."

It was a good reminder to the other men, but Quinlan didn't really need it. For him, no mission was routine. His heart pounded a hundred beats a minute as he constantly scanned the area, settling his eyes back on Sir Baylor after each sweep. The hours melted away slowly, and fatigue settled in. Had the assault been called off?

He scanned once more and suddenly saw the commander signal. The enemy was approaching. Quinlan's stomach rose to his throat as he drew his sword. He scanned his assigned region more quickly, not wanting to miss any of the commander's signals.

Next came the direction—southeast, as predicted. Kessler and Drake would be ready. Quinlan couldn't help but breathe a little easier.

Another scan, another signal. Three Shadow Warriors were coming—one less than expected. This also made Quinlan feel better...until he realized it could mean trouble elsewhere.

He looked once more toward Baylor for the signal to relocate, but it did not come. Instead, Baylor motioned for Purcell to join Kessler and Drake.

Quinlan was confused. This was not the rehearsed sequence. He made one more scan and looked back to Baylor, but he was too late to catch the last signal. Then the commander disappeared.

Quinlan watched as Kessler, Drake, and Purcell disappeared from their posts, preparing for the fight. He looked for Baylor to give the signal again, but there was no sign of him.

What had Quinlan missed? What was he supposed to do? If he stayed where he was but had been called to join the others, they might be outnumbered. If he left his post but had been signaled to stay, warriors might slip through into the haven. He began to pace, trying to decide which course of action would result in the least disastrous ramification.

Finally he could wait no more. He ran toward Kessler and Drake's last known position. Halfway there, he heard the clash of an intense duel. Quinlan gripped his sword tighter and quickened his pace, hoping he had judged correctly. He was nearly to the fight when he heard another clash of steel behind him.

Quinlan stopped in his tracks. Through the sparse woods he saw Kessler, Drake, and Purcell locked in deadly battle against three massive Shadow Warriors. Dread filled his heart as he realized Sir Baylor was probably also engaged. He ran the last few paces and came upon Purcell's fight first.

"What are you doing?" Purcell screamed at Quinlan in between blows. "Baylor ordered you to stay at your post!"

Quinlan spun on his heels and raced back to where he had been. The sound of a desperate fight filled the air, and Quinlan hoped against hope that he was not too late to help. He climbed a small rise and looked down the other side to see Sir Baylor engaged with two warriors. One more was just joining the fray.

Quinlan froze as he realized the hopelessness of the situation. Baylor was seriously outnumbered, and Quinlan could not possibly cover the ground between them in time to help. Quinlan screamed and began to run as a Shadow Warrior plunged his sword deep into Sir Baylor's side and the other two added their swords to the dreadful act.

Baylor's sword fell to the ground. The Shadow Warriors withdrew their swords. Baylor collapsed to his knees, then fell face forward.

Rage boiled up in Quinlan's heart as he closed in with sword raised, not caring for his own life. One of the Shadow Warriors bent over Sir Baylor while the other two turned toward Quinlan. It was then that he noted their bizarre black and green painted faces and the thin bands of black cloth across their eyes. They raised their swords toward Quinlan, but before he could engage them he heard the pounding of horses' hoofs behind him.

Kessler, Drake, and Purcell thundered past Quinlan. The Shadow Warriors retreated, and the knights pursued them. Quinlan fell to his knees beside Sir Baylor and turned him onto his back.

Baylor winced and gasped, blood trickling down from his mouth to his chin.

"I'm sorry, Commander, I didn't—"

"Quinlan," Baylor rasped urgently, "Take this…" He reached for the disk that hung about his neck, snapped the silver chain, and pressed the coin-shaped object into Quinlan's hand.

Quinlan shook his head, fighting back tears.

"Take it…I didn't"—Baylor coughed, and his eyes grew wide in pain—"choose you…you were…"

It was too much. The evil of Lucius had done its work, and Baylor closed his eyes in death.

"No…no…no!" Quinlan buried his head in his hands and leaned forward against Baylor's chest. He screamed against the reality of his error and would have died to change it. Time refused to go on as Quinlan wallowed in the agony of the moment. But gradually, between his own moans he became aware of cries and screams in the distance.

Quinlan lifted his head and listened. The haven of Garriston and the people there were under attack, while Kessler, Drake, and Purcell were pursuing Baylor's killers in the opposite direction.

Quinlan jumped to his feet and ran to Kobalt. Not waiting for his fellow knights, he galloped toward Garriston. He arrived to find the chaos of a full assault on the knights, men, women, and children of the haven. The camp buildings and barns were ablaze, and more than twenty dark warriors on horseback were raining death upon anyone who was accessible. The few haven knights who remained on their feet were engaged in the fight of their lives.

Quinlan galloped to join the fight, aching for vengeance against those who had been responsible for his commander's death. He engaged the first warrior he met and noticed immediately that something was different about him and his comrades. They wore the same ghostly black and green face paint Quinlan had seen on two of the warriors who killed Baylor. They were smaller than the Shadow Warriors the valor knights had fought at Arimil and wore more tightly fitting armor. Quinlan wondered if these were the Vincero Knights he had heard about—Arrethtraens who fought for Lucius—but their markings clearly identified them as Shadow Warriors.

Quinlan crosscut and thrust, then parried and countered. The warrior fought without expression, neither cursing nor shouting.

Quinlan caught a vertical cut, countered and thrust. This time his sword found its mark, and it penetrated deep into his enemy's side.

He hesitated just a moment for the invasion of his blade to take its effect, but that was a mistake. The warrior's face did not change, and his blade returned toward Quinlan with the speed and force of a whole man.

Quinlan could not recover in time. He withdrew his sword and raised his left arm, catching the edge of the warrior's sword with the vambrace on his forearm. The force of the blow carried on through to his shoulder and knocked him off Kobalt.

He hit the ground with a thud. By the time he regained his feet, his opponent had launched his steed toward an unsuspecting woman. The evil warrior struck her down, then turned and looked at Quinlan once more. There was no smile, no sneer, no curse—just the face of undeterred evil that could never be satisfied.

The Shadow Warrior turned and attacked him once more. Quinlan was now at an extreme disadvantage, for his enemy was mounted and he was not. He prepared himself to take the blow from above, then realized the warrior's intention was simply to trample him under the massive steed he rode.

Quinlan dove to his left, narrowly missing the animal's deadly hoofs. The warrior wheeled and charged again, this time swinging his sword for a final deathblow. Quinlan feigned another dive, but instead thrust his sword up through the belly of the warrior's horse. He lost his grip on his sword as the animal reared, screamed, and collapsed to the ground, sending its rider tumbling.

Quinlan drew his long knife and dove on top of the rattled warrior before he could regain his feet. Leather and steel entangled as the two combatants fought for an advantage. The warrior slammed an elbow into Quinlan's jaw, and the young knight nearly lost his senses. He countered with a gauntleted fist that tore off the thin band of black cloth that hid the warrior's eyes.

Chills ran up Quinlan's spine as he stared into his enemy's eyes. He felt as though he had just peered into the empty cavern of an ocean abyss. There was nothing there…no life, no soul.

The warrior squinted in the light, and this gave Quinlan the opportunity he needed. His long knife pierced through a chink in the warrior's armor, and the warrior went still. This time Quinlan did not hesitate. He withdrew the knife and lunged for his sword, which lay near the body of the fallen steed. He scrambled to get a solid grip on the handle, for other warriors were coming his way.

Quinlan sprinted a few paces away to avoid the leading warriors and their horses, but to his surprise, they raced past him and beyond into the surrounding woods. The remaining warriors gave up their grim work and followed. There was no battle cry of victory or taunting of future evil deeds, just the silent exodus of a merciless enemy.

He glanced toward the warrior he had defeated and was shocked to see him rising to his feet. The warrior stumbled, then gathered himself and ran toward one of the last retreating warriors. The mounted warrior reached down, locked hands, and swung Quinlan's foe onto the back of his horse, and they disappeared into the dust stirred up by their retreating comrades.

Breathing hard, Quinlan stood and surveyed the destruction around him. A few Silent Warriors had been killed, but many more men, women, and children lay motionless. Moments later, Kessler, Drake, and Purcell rushed into the aftermath and dismounted near him, swords drawn and ready.

Kessler and Drake looked all around them, trying to make sense of what had happened, but Purcell came straight for Quinlan.

"He signaled you to stay!" Purcell rushed at Quinlan and shoved him backward. "They had split their forces and were coming in your direction. You left the commander open to an ambush!"

Tears filled Quinlan's eyes. All he could do was slowly shake his head. He had no words to defend, deny, or excuse himself.

"That's enough, Purcell." Kessler stepped between them. Purcell glared at Kessler, then spun about and walked a few paces away.

Quinlan looked into Kessler's eyes and saw the same pain and disappointment that he felt in his own heart. Drake silently turned away, obviously wrestling with his own anger. Quinlan hung his head in utter shame.

"Can you help us?" a voice called out. A knight approached them, carrying a child. Blood spilled from a gash on his head.

"The buildings are lost, and we have many wounded. We can take them over there." He motioned with his head to a clearing away from the burning buildings.

His appearance jarred the knights from their own grief and anger. "What…happened?" Drake asked slowly.

The man shook his head. "We knew there was a threat, but this is far beyond anything we expected." He turned and looked sadly at the remnants of the haven. "I've seen Shadow Warriors before," he said solemnly. "These were something…more. Some of my people will ask where the Prince was in all of this." He shook his head again, then proceeded on to the clearing where others were gathering.

For the rest of the day, the four valor knights lost themselves in the duties of giving aid. They transported the wounded to homes in the city and stayed until there was little more they could do. At one point,

Quinlan found himself tending a severely wounded young knight in the haven leader's home.

"I saw you fight that warrior," the young man said. "I hope I can be as brave as you one day."

Quinlan clenched his teeth. The boy's comments stung like salt in a fresh wound. "There is only One whose actions you should aspire to duplicate," he said quietly.

The young man smiled. "The Prince!" Then he closed his eyes to rest.

Quinlan exited the house and started down the street, but he stopped when he heard voices around the corner. Drake, Purcell, and Kessler were discussing their options.

"So you want to just give up and ride away?" That was Kessler. "The Swords of Valor are to be no more?"

"Taras only spoke to the commander," Purcell's voice replied. "We are part of this unit because Baylor recruited us. How are we supposed to continue without him?"

Silence.

"Well?"

"I'm afraid he's right," Drake finally said.

"What of Quinlan?" Kessler asked.

"What of him?" Purcell's voice was bitter. "I knew that bringing him into the unit was a mistake. Now Baylor has paid for it with his life!"

Purcell's words hit Quinlan square in the chest, and he could take it no more. The muscles convulsed on his burning face as he quietly moved away from the corner, found Kobalt, and silently disappeared into the night.

NINE

PATHYON

"Baylor is dead, my lord, and the Swords of Valor have disbanded." The bald Shadow Warrior bowed low before the dark throne of Lucius as he gave his report. "My paythas are quickly reproducing and making imbeciles out of the Knights of the Prince."

A wicked smile crossed the Dark Lord's face, and he turned to the massive figure beside him. "See, Luskan. Pathyon is exactly who we needed for Burkfield." His smiled turned to a scowl. "Don't ever hesitate on my orders again!"

"Yes, my lord." The massive Shadow Warrior said. "But may I remind your lordship that it was my Assassin Warriors that executed Baylor, not Pathyon and his furry—"

"Quit sniveling, Luskan," Lucius growled. "Your drugged warrior squad may have killed Baylor for us, but I need warriors whose minds aren't turned to mush when you're through with them."

Luskan shot Pathyon a vengeful glare, but Pathyon ignored it.

"With the Swords of Valor disbanded and my paythas controlling the haven knights, destroying Burkfield will be rather simple. Shall I proceed?" Pathyon's dark eyes gleamed in anticipation of the carnage.

"Not yet. We shall fatten the calf before we kill it and feast." Lucius brought his hands together and crossed his fingers. "Let the city continue to prosper and the haven slowly die. Then I will make an example of that city for all of the kingdom to see. Its destruction will help initiate my final plan."

"As you wish, my lord." Pathyon bowed low once more and smiled as he exited the dark throne room. Luskan scowled at him as he exited. In an empire built on deception and treachery, there are no friends.

TEN

TWITCH ONCE MORE

Quinlan spurred Kobalt hard, trying to put distance between them and what happened at Garriston, but there was no escaping. With every mile he felt the reality of it closing in, draining him of hope.

A storm threatened on the Plains of Zoat, but Quinlan barely noticed. Lightning arced from cloud to cloud in a constant strobe of brilliant flashes, but he rode on. When the dark clouds overhead roared and poured rain down on him, it felt only right.

Quinlan had been riding for hours when he finally stopped Kobalt and slid to the ground. He stumbled away from the steed and on through torrential downpour, conscious of nothing but his agonizing thoughts.

He had been insignificant his whole life. And now his feeble effort to follow the Prince under Sir Baylor's tutelage felt like a mockery. Baylor was dead. The Swords of Valor blamed Quinlan, and justifiably so. He had dared to care and now desperately wished he hadn't, for the pain was unbearable.

He fell to his knees in the mud and buried his face in his hands. His tears disappeared into the streams of rainwater that flowed down his face. Quinlan was certain that no one in all the land would care or notice if he simply vanished. If only he could do just that.

"What a fool I was even to try," he said aloud, but the thunder robbed him of even this small moment of mourning. He ached to the very depth of his soul and could not imagine the pain ever stopping.

I'm sorry, my Prince. Who am I to think that I could serve You? I am... nothing.

Long after the rain had stopped, Quinlan still crouched in the mud, unable to move. Kobalt came over and nudged him, then nudged again. After three attempts, the horse managed to stir his master. Quinlan grabbed onto his steed's harness and lifted himself up. With monumental effort, he managed to mount. Then, with hardly a thought, he set his course toward Burkfield.

On the long journey home, Quinlan avoided all human contact, for the only comfort he found in his grief was his isolation. His travel was extremely slow, and he had to subsist on nuts and berries, but he didn't care. He didn't even really care if he made it home—in fact, he dreaded it. He only traveled that direction because it *was* a direction.

After two weeks of travel, an emaciated Quinlan finally arrived in Burkfield.

"Twitch!" Tav shouted when he opened the door and Quinlan nearly fell through it. "What in the kingdom happened to you?"

Tav grabbed his friend and helped him to a chair. He brought him a flask of water, some bread, and some fruit and waited patiently while Quinlan slowly ate and drank.

"Thank you," Quinlan said softly.

By now, Tav's father and mother had joined them. All were relieved to see Quinlan but obviously concerned for him. Tav's father crossed his arms across his chest. "Is Baylor nearby?"

Quinlan shook his head. He didn't yet have the courage to tell them what had happened. "I'm very tired," he murmured.

"Of course," Tav's mother said. "Your room is just as it was."

Quinlan gave her a thankful nod and stumbled down the hallway. Maybe this time sleep would bring him relief.

After a few days of recovery, Quinlan was finally able to share the tragic news of Sir Baylor's death with Tav and his parents. They took it better than Quinlan had expected. He wondered if perhaps they tempered their response for his sake, for he could hardly speak the words of that dreadful story. They also seemed hesitant to believe him, for that would mean believing that Baylor was more than a fanatic.

For Quinlan, the memory of that tragic day in Garriston was a wound that wouldn't heal, for he kept reliving every detail in his mind. The pain of the memory seemed an appropriate penance for his gross error, a small price to pay for the life of one as great as Sir Baylor and the damage to the work of the Prince in Arrethtrae. He tortured himself with wondering how many Knights of the Prince were attempting missions unprotected by the Swords of Valor. That thought also caused him to wonder why he had never seen attacks made on the haven or city of Burkfield.

As the weeks and months passed, Quinlan's questions gradually faded into the background and he began to live days that were not completely filled with regret. He eased back into his old life at Burkfield and became Twitch once more.

Even as the pain of his error slowly faded, however, he found himself unable to find peace in his old life. He had seen the other side of the kingdom, both the dark and the glorious, and no matter how comfortable he was in Burkfield, he couldn't forget that ancient hidden war. Caught between two worlds, he was more miserable than he had ever been in his life.

Tav wasn't much help. He and Quinlan tried to pick up their friendship where they had left off, but both had changed. Disty, now the size of a raccoon and an ever-present companion to Tav, was a constant irritant to Quinlan. Since his commissioning, Tav had also begun spending more time with Mirya and less time at the haven.

For different reasons, Quinlan was reticent in regard to his involvement with the Burkfield haven, and Sir Edmund did not press the issue. He assigned Quinlan to maintenance and other menial tasks required at the haven, a job that suited his carpentry skills quite well. On the surface, it seemed a natural fit for Twitch. Inwardly, Quinlan was slowly dying.

Quinlan knew Sir Edmund was a good man, though frustrated by the growing lack of enthusiasm among many of the Followers at the haven. Quinlan occasionally felt the urge to help but couldn't bring himself to step forward for anything more than a routine presence. Discouragement had closed up his ears to any call to missions.

About four months after Quinlan's journey back to Burkfield, word began to spread that a man of renown would be visiting in an effort to revitalize the haven. Mixed emotions welled up in Quinlan when he heard the visitor's name—Sir Worthington. The man and his supporting knights would conduct a week's worth of special training.

Although originally from Cameria, Quinlan was told, the man worked out of the haven at Thecia, planning and conducting missions. His significant success as a servant of the Prince had earned him kingdom-wide attention in recent months. He was a man everyone wanted to meet...or almost everyone.

"Are you going to attend the meetings?" Quinlan asked Tav one morning at breakfast.

"I've got other plans...with Mirya." Tav winked at Quinlan. "You'll have to tell me how it goes."

"Sure." Quinlan looked sadly at his friend, who seemed to be slipping away from the call of the Prince.

Quinlan wasn't sure he wanted to attend the training either, but he was curious about Sir Worthington. He had liked the man from their brief encounter but wondered how all the prestige had changed him. Such widespread fame was like having a porcupine for a pet—eventually you're going to get pierced. Quinlan also wondered how much of Worthington's recognition was due to his natural charisma and how much was due to truly doing the work of the Prince. Would the Swords of Valor still be defending him if they hadn't disbanded?

Quinlan decided to attend the first day of training just to see if Worthington was worth the effort of defending him.

Quinlan arrived at the haven that day to find only twenty-four knights had gathered for the first session—a paltry showing for a city the size of Burkfield. Sir Worthington was already addressing them, and Quinlan found an inconspicuous place at the back where he could pretend to work on a broken segment of a fence while he watched and listened.

Six of Worthington's supporting knights, four male and two female knights, stood near the front. Quinlan watched them first, knowing he could learn much about Worthington by observing those who followed him. The knights looked confident and serious. One of them was the female knight he remembered from Arimil.

Quinlan then turned his attention to the stately looking Sir Worthington, who addressed the assembly with a gentle but compelling voice. "Each of you is here for his or her own reason. Some are here because you are simply curious." Quinlan felt his cheeks flush as Worthington continued. "Some are here because it would look bad if you weren't. Others have come because you truly want to develop your skills as knights."

Worthington smiled as several in his audience nodded. "Whatever your reason, I am glad you are here. I hope that when we are through, all of you will be here for only one reason—because you want to serve the King and the Prince with your whole heart! Without that as your reason, you are not truly a knight."

Worthington drew his sword and placed the tip in the ground before him. "Sir Edmund asked me to come, but you must understand that I come at great risk to you." He paused to let the knights absorb his words. "The Dark Knight is out there, and he will stop at nothing to destroy the cause of the Prince."

He picked up the sword and swept its tip in front of him. "My fellow knights, the cause of the Prince is your cause too. When your heart pounds with passion for that cause, you take up a battle that has been raging from the beginning of time."

Quinlan's eyes suddenly filled, and he turned away. He was unprepared for the powerful tug those words made on his heart.

"You wear the mark of the Prince," Worthington continued. "He died on a tree so that you each could become one of His knights. Do not let the comforts of this kingdom distract you from the call he gave Cedric, William, Rob, and the other first knights on that great day. We are called to go into all the kingdom and recruit others to become Knights of the Prince, stay true to the Code, and prepare for battle against the Dark Knight. And I ask, are you prepared to do that?"

Worthington looked across the assembly, gazing into the eyes of each knight. Quinlan took a deep breath, feeling foolish and self-righteous for presuming to judge Sir Worthington. He wanted to leave but couldn't…not yet. He needed to hear and see more.

Sir Worthington and his knights broke up the assembly into smaller units to dig more deeply into the Code. Quinlan busied himself with a few camp duties but listened in on a session that a knight was conducting nearby.

"Understand that the Code was perfectly fulfilled by the Prince," the knight said with enthusiasm, "something no Arrethtraen could ever do. Because of the King's great Son, the Code is therefore written on our hearts, and we live in the spirit of the Code, a governing that transcends rules written on parchment."

Quinlan was amazed at the quality of Worthington's training. He fully understood why Sir Edmund had sent for the man and his team. He also wondered if, in the absence of the Swords of Valor, the Silent Warriors were working harder to protect Worthington. Had Quinlan's error actually put this great man in danger?

Eventually Worthington and his knights began training the knights from the haven in various methods of combat, especially sword fighting. Fear of failure kept Quinlan from joining, and knowledge of the truth kept him from leaving, but by noon the conflict in his bosom was more than he could take.

Turning to leave, he collided directly with one of Worthington's knights—the young woman he had seen in Arimil.

"Sorry," Quinlan mumbled and backed up a step.

The young knight stared at him with beautiful blue eyes that seemed to sparkle with life, even though her countenance was quite serious. "It's all right," she replied, pushing a loose tendril of dark brown hair out of her face. The rest of it was gathered in a braid that hung midway down her back. "It's not the first time."

Quinlan stared at her. Up close she was even more striking than Quinlan had thought, and the sight of her threw him into confusion. In times past, this is where Tav would have taken over and Quinlan would willingly have retreated and watched. But Tav was not here, and Quinlan looked desperately for a quick and easy exit.

"So," the woman asked, "what's your story?"

"I...well...I..." Quinlan fumbled for words. "What do you mean?"

"Well, you've been here since early this morning but haven't once joined in on the training." She flashed him a teasing smile. "Is your sword broken?"

"You could say that, I guess." Quinlan felt his cheek tense, and he instinctively put up his hand to rub it.

The young woman stared straight into his eyes, all teasing gone. "Do you have any idea what's really going on here?"

Stunned by the change in her demeanor, Quinlan couldn't speak or look away. Slowly he nodded.

"Then what are you afraid of?"

At that Quinlan's cheek went into spasms. "Excuse me," he said and turned toward the stables to find Kobalt. As he walked, he heard Worthington's voice far behind him.

"Raisa, we are here to train and recruit. You're not supposed to chase our knights away!"

"Time is short," Quinlan heard the woman reply. "The ones who stay will truly care about serving the Prince. We both know it takes more than wearing a tunic with His mark!"

Quinlan's first response was to quicken his pace, but then he stopped. He had been ridiculed by handsome people his whole life, and he was tired of it. He turned on his heel and met the challenge of those intense blue eyes with an angry glare of his own. He didn't care how pretty she was. He had had enough.

The moment was brief, but Quinlan saw her flinch even from this distance. He turned back and resumed his walk to the stables.

"He looks familiar. Do we know him?" Quinlan heard Worthington say reflectively.

"Not that I'm aware," she answered, then raised her voice to make sure Quinlan heard. "But if he's brave enough, perhaps he'll come back tomorrow!"

"What *am* I going to do with you, Raisa?" Quinlan heard Worthington say.

ELEVEN

JOURNEY TO NOWHERE

 Quinlan watched Disty scurry up and down the shoreline of Jewel Lake, scouting for fish. He was glad the creature was away from Tav at least for a few moments. He had an announcement to make.

"I'm leaving town," Quinlan said as he cast his line in from the shoreline.

Tav made a face. "Twitch, I know I haven't spent much time with you since you've been back, but you shouldn't run off and do something rash again."

"This isn't rash, and it has nothing to do with you, Tav." Quinlan looked at his childhood friend. "I made a commitment to the Prince, and for a short time I found real purpose in waking up each morning. Then when your uncle died, everything collapsed in on me." Quinlan looked out across serene waters that sparkled in the early spring sunshine. "I thought I could return to my life here, but I'm more miserable now than I've ever been."

"I just think you're getting too worked up about being a knight." Tav relaxed against a boulder and sighed with satisfaction. "Look, the Prince wants what's best for us, right? What's wrong with being comfortable and enjoying life a little?"

"You don't understand, Tav. I'm miserable because I know I'm not serving the Prince as I should be. I feel I'm just wasting away while others are doing my work." He picked up a small stone and threw it into the lake.

"Hey," Tav scolded. "Don't scare the fish."

Quinlan laid down his fishing pole and turned to face Tav. "Why don't you come with me? Remember when we said we'd ride together into the kingdom on grand missions for the Prince? Tav, you're twice the knight I am. Imagine what we could accomplish together. There's a war raging out there, and we could make a difference. What do you say?"

Tav seemed lost in thought as he considered Quinlan's proposal. Disty, seeming to sense his master's contemplation, scurried up next to him and chortled softly. Tav shook his head quickly as if waking from a dream, then let loose a laugh.

"You're starting to sound as crazy as Baylor, chum." Tav pulled in his line to recast. "Why would you ever want to leave Burkfield?" His line flew out into the lake and plunked into the cold blue water.

In that moment, Quinlan realized he was a man without a home…and without a friend who really understood him. The truth was, he didn't understand Tav anymore either.

Quinlan got to his feet. "Thanks for letting me stay with you these past months."

Tav looked up at Quinlan. "You really are going, aren't you?"

"Yes," Quinlan replied sadly.

Tav looked perturbed. "You're chasing a dream that doesn't exist, Twitch."

"I don't believe that, but if it's true, at least I'm chasing something."

He walked a few steps, then turned back. "By the way, my name's Quinlan."

Within an hour, Quinlan had packed Kobalt and was riding south. He had little money, no destination, and no plans, just an intense desire to find purpose once more in his life. His experience with the Swords of

Valor had ended tragically, but it had also shown him what it was like truly to live. Quinlan knew that kind of life could be found only in serving the Prince.

When Burkfield was nearly out of sight, Quinlan turned and looked at the country he had called home for so long. Mount Resolute rose up tall out of the landscape, a reminder of the commitment Quinlan had made one strange autumn eve.

Over the next few days, Quinlan meandered south from village to village until he came to the town of Kurryvale on the southern coast. The chilly spring day was made miserable by a spitting mist that threatened to turn into a full rain. By the time he had reached the outskirts of the town, he was chilled to the bone and looking forward to a fire and a meal. He hoped the town had an inn.

As Kobalt trotted along the empty road, Quinlan noticed a dark lump next to a tree near the ditch—perhaps a forgotten gunnysack that had spilled from a wagon. But as he passed, he heard a cough and a wheeze—or thought he heard it. He hesitated, but the lump didn't move.

Quinlan shivered and rode on, telling himself he had been mistaken. He spotted the town inn partway down the main thoroughfare and picked up his pace, but after passing the first set of shops, he pulled back on the reins. Kobalt nickered as if to question why they had stopped shy of their destination.

Quinlan turned in the saddle and looked back down the road. Then he sighed, turned the horse around, and made his way back to the tree. He dismounted and peered more closely at the dark shape. He heard another cough.

He approached cautiously, wary of being taken by a roadway thief. "Are you all right, sir?" he called while still a couple of paces away.

The man didn't move.

"I say, are you all right, sir?"

Slowly the man turned his head to peer out from the tattered blanket he had wrapped around himself. His face was deathly pale. Quinlan drew nearer and knelt before the man on the wet grass.

"Do you live here?" he asked. "Is there somewhere I can take you?"

The man slowly shook his head and began coughing again. Recovering from the coughing fit seemed to take nearly every bit of his remaining strength.

Quinlan looked up and down the road for someone else to offer some help, but he and the man were alone.

"What's your name, sir?" he asked.

"Terrance." The man's voice was a hoarse whisper. He looked to be about forty years old, though in his condition it was hard to tell. Matted brown hair hung about his eyes.

"Come, Terrance. Let's get you someplace dry." Quinlan put an arm around the man to help him up. The man shivered uncontrollably.

Terrance held onto Quinlan's arm and the tree to stand up. Quinlan led him to Kobalt and helped him into the saddle. He then led Kobalt to the inn and ushered the man through the doors. An enticing fire burned in the fireplace. Quinlan looked about and saw a red-faced, heavyset woman looking sternly their way.

"Madam, this man needs—"

"Don't harbor no plague victims here," she said.

"He just needs some food and a place to lie down," Quinlan explained.

The woman put her hands on her hips and eyed Terrance closely.

"You got money to pay?" she asked Quinlan.

He nodded, and she exchanged the concern in her countenance for sympathy. "Why don't you take him to that table near the fire so he can dry up some."

Quinlan guided Terrance to the table and set him in a chair. The fire was as pleasing and as warm as it looked. Before long, the innkeeper returned with a loaf of bread and two bowls of hot chestnut soup. At first Terrance couldn't even get his own spoon to his lips, so Quinlan fed him the first half of his bowl of soup. With each spoonful, however, Terrance seemed to regain some of his strength, and his shivering gradually went away.

Quinlan dipped the spoon into the bowl once more, but Terrance reached out and put his hand on Quinlan's. "Thank you, sir." He took the spoon from Quinlan and brought it to his lips, careful not to spill a single drop. He closed his eyes as he slurped the soup from the spoon.

Quinlan let the man focus on the task of eating and turned his attention to his own bowl. It wasn't the best he'd ever tasted, but the warmth in his stomach felt good. He tore off a nice-sized portion of bread and held it out for Terrance. Terrance looked at Quinlan as if he couldn't believe someone would be so kind to him. Tears welled up in his eyes as he took the bread.

Quinlan tore a piece for himself and dunked it into the soup. The bread softened and quickly soaked up the seasoned soup. To Quinlan it tasted wonderful. When he finished, he excused himself and sought out the innkeeper.

"Do you have any rooms, madam?"

She crinkled her nose as she looked at Quinlan. "I've rooms. It'll be one florin a night, and there's only one bed per room."

Quinlan paid the woman for two rooms, returned to the table, and sat down again across from Terrance, who had just finished his soup. "Why are you helping me?" he asked.

Quinlan mustered a smile. "I am a Knight of the Prince, and this is what we do."

Quinlan wished he could give him more, but right now he felt like as much of a misplaced wanderer as Terrance looked.

Terrance bowed his head for a moment, then looked up at Quinlan. "Wherever you are going, good sir, know that the kingdom needs more of you. May the King's joy be your own and His protection follow you wherever you are bound."

Quinlan stared at Terrance and suddenly felt like he was the one being ministered to. That blessing eased the ache in his heart in a way the man would never know. He smiled and lowered his head.

"Where *are* you bound, sir, that I should be so favored as to receive your kindness this day?" Terrance asked. His eyes seemed full of woe and fatigue, yet he was asking about Quinlan. Perhaps the conversation was a distraction from Terrance's own life of obvious sorrow.

"I'm not sure," Quinlan replied. "I think perhaps it isn't so much where I'm bound as what I'm leaving behind."

"Ah." Terrance nodded as if he understood, then turned to face the fire. His whole body shivered once more as he spread his hands to catch the warmth. "I've learned that when I quit looking behind me, I quit stumbling over that which lies before me," he said as he stared into the licking flames.

Quinlan tilted his head, thinking Terrance was not the typical homeless vagabond. "Where are you from?" he asked.

Terrance closed his eyes. "So many places I can't remember, but the castle of Ironheart was my last place of duty."

"You're a proper man, Terrance," Quinlan said. "What's happened to you?"

Terrance hesitated a long while.

"I was betrayed," he finally said. He tried to take a deep breath, but a coughing fit cut it short. By the time he stopped coughing, he looked ready to fall over from complete exhaustion.

"Come, Terrance." Quinlan helped the man to his feet. "I've a room for you upstairs."

Terrance leaned into Quinlan's strength. "Thank you," he whispered.

That night, Quinlan slept peacefully for the first time in many weeks. The following morning, he awoke to a window full of sunshine, ready for another day's journey.

He checked in on Terrance and was pleased to see the man sleeping soundly. After paying for a couple of meals and another night's stay for Terrance, he left instructions for the innkeeper to check in on Terrance once he left. Then he found a table near the door of the inn, settled into a worn wooden chair, and ordered breakfast.

He was leaning across the table to swat at a fly when something hard pressed against his ribs. He reached inside a pocket in his doublet, then froze when his fingers found the source of the discomfort—something that confused, saddened, and excited him all at the same time.

He slowly pulled the object from his doublet.

TWELVE

THE CRYSTAL COIN

 Quinlan fingered the medallion and marveled once again at its beauty. As he lifted it closer to his eyes, the broken silver chain fell to the table. He returned the chain to his pocket but kept the disk out for further inspection.

Until now, the medallion had been difficult for Quinlan even to look at because it was a reminder of Sir Baylor and the last few moments of his life. Now, with some time between him and that dreadful day, Quinlan began to inspect the masterful work of art with a different perspective. At close range, it looked like…a crystal coin.

The outer rim was silver, with an inlaid gold design that gleamed in the light of the nearby lanterns. The inner disk was colorless crystal with prism cuts around the edge and a flat, clear center. Quinlan looked through it and realized the image beneath was slightly magnified.

Why did Sir Baylor give this to me? Quinlan wondered. *What was so important about it that he spent the last few moments of his life making sure he gave it to someone?*

Quinlan placed his thumb beneath the edge and flipped the coin into the air. He watched as the light of the inn lanterns streamed through the crystal in a moving arc of brilliant color. Quinlan flipped the coin a few more times, varying the speed at which the coin rotated, mesmerized by the colorful effect.

Two men entered the inn, walked to the table in the far corner, and sat down. One of them wore a hood pulled over his head. The other looked nervously from table to table, and Quinlan could tell some shady deal was in the making—an arrangement to trade illegal goods or perhaps a weapons and arms deal. Either way, there was nothing Quinlan could do about it. He had been reduced to a spectator in a kingdom full of contradiction.

He scanned the inn's tables once more without looking or thinking about anything in particular. The hooded man was now leaning forward, pointing a finger at his tablemate.

Quinlan flipped the crystal coin in the air once more. It slowly turned end over end, flying to the exact height of Quinlan's right eye and intersecting his line of sight to the men in the corner. As the coin completed one rotation, his gaze passed through the aligned glass of the crystal coin. In that one brief instant, Quinlan saw something that made the hair on his neck stand up. A faint aura of green light emanated from the body of the hooded man.

Quinlan snatched the coin before it could fall back to his hand. Had he really seen what he thought he saw? He had looked through the crystal before and seen nothing unusual.

"Two eggs and mash." The server plopped down a plate, interrupting Quinlan's discovery. "You want ale or water?"

"Water, please," Quinlan said.

The server poured a goblet full of water as Quinlan looked back at the corner table. He saw the nervous man scan the room again, and Quinlan feigned being preoccupied with his food. When they were locked in conversation again, Quinlan brought the coin to his eye and looked through the clear crystal. Everything looked completely normal except for the hooded man. The faint aura of green light was no trick upon the eyes. The man's entire body glowed, and the light was brighter at the openings of the cloak, around his gloved hands and covered face.

Quinlan's heart began to race as he considered what this might mean. Just then, the hooded man looked straight at Quinlan. Though covered by the hood, his glowing green face was as clear as if there were no hood at all, and his eyes glowed a brilliant green. They spewed hatred in a way that shook Quinlan to the bone.

He quickly pulled the coin from his eye to see the blackened shadow of the hooded face turned his direction. There was no doubt in Quinlan's mind what the hooded figure was.

Quinlan's heart pounded hard in his chest, and his stomach rose up to his throat. He tried to swallow but couldn't. He looked down at his food, trying to look indifferent, but a moment later he looked back at the men. The hooded figure was still staring at him.

Quinlan put a few coins on the table, stood, and walked to the door as nonchalantly as possible. Once outside, he started running, but before he had gone twenty paces, the door to the inn burst open, and the hooded man stepped out. He quickly spotted Quinlan and gave chase.

Quinlan's fear was now fully confirmed, and he looked for some way to escape the Shadow Warrior's pursuit. He didn't know what this evil vassal of Lucius had in mind, but he was sure it couldn't be good.

There was no time to tack up Kobalt and get away, so Quinlan ran past the stables toward the shops beyond. He dodged down the first street and ran as fast as his feet would take him. He turned back to see that the Shadow Warrior had made the corner too and was gaining on him.

Up ahead was a crowd of people buying produce at an open market. Quinlan dodged quickly between the people, trying desperately to put some distance between himself and his pursuer. He looked over his shoulder again and could see that the man was frustrated by the crowd and the need to be somewhat discreet.

Quinlan ducked into a shoemaker's shop and found a full shelf of shoes to hide behind. He peered through the shoes toward the street and watched as the Shadow Warrior passed by, continuing his search farther down the street.

Quinlan pulled the crystal coin from his pocket and looked at it once more. "Where did Baylor get you?" he murmured.

"Wanting a fine pair of shoes?" a voice behind him asked.

"Just looking today." Quinlan told the shoemaker. He walked to the door and stepped out carefully, looking in the direction he'd seen the Shadow Warrior travel. Turning back toward the inn, he found himself face to face with the man who had been sitting across from the Shadow Warrior.

"I think my associate wants to speak with you." The man leered and tilted his head to the side as if to look over Quinlan's shoulder. Quinlan turned his head and saw the Shadow Warrior standing just behind him. A large hand gripped his shoulder, and he felt the tip of a dagger at his back. "Come with me," the dark voice said close to his ear.

Quinlan wanted to call for help, but even in this crowd of people he knew there was no one who could stand against a Shadow Warrior. Why would they even try? No one here knew Quinlan.

The warrior pushed Quinlan down the street and into a deserted alley, never relinquishing his grip. With every step, Quinlan fully expected the dagger to make its plunge into his back. He had to try something, even if it was a pointless and desperate action. With the next step, he twisted his body and fell away from the dagger while reaching for his sword. With a quick somersault, he recovered to one knee and held his sword before him.

Quinlan was pleased the move had worked but fully expected the Shadow Warrior's blade to plummet toward his head. What he saw instead was the warrior just standing before him in silence. Quinlan pushed to his feet as the warrior sheathed the dagger and then lifted the hood from his head and let it fall to his back.

Quinlan gaped at what he saw. The warrior's face was grotesquely scarred, as was a large section of his skull on the left side where no hair grew.

"Give me the kasilite medallion." The warrior's voice was deep and dark.

Another voice spoke. "Can I have his money and sword?" Quinlan glanced to the side and saw the other man from the inn.

"Shut up, Victor!" The warrior scolded, then held out his hand. "The medallion."

Quinlan gripped his sword tightly. "I don't know what you mean."

The warrior slowly lifted the left portion of his cloak back over his shoulder and drew his sword. "I can either kill you and take it, or you can give it to me and I may not kill you. Either way, I *will* have it."

Quinlan gulped but held fast to the sword, sending up a silent plea for help. Somewhere inside he found the courage to speak the words that he had been taught would summon Silent Warriors to his aid: "The King reigns…and His Son!"

The warrior cringed at the words and glanced from side to side, then sneered and raised his sword.

"Looks like you will die alone." He pulled back to strike but hesitated. Quinlan heard hoofbeats coming up the alley behind him. Had the Silent Warriors heard him? He wanted to look but dared not take his eyes from the warrior in front of him.

"Ah, Gravicus, what have you found here?"

Quinlan took a couple of steps back from the scarred warrior and turned to see who had come to his aid. Two large warriors dismounted and strode toward them. Quinlan's relief turned to confusion as the scarred warrior replied, "Go away, Yin, and leave him to me. There's nothing here for you."

"What's he after, Victor?" the warrior named Yin asked the man behind Gravicus. Victor's nervous mannerisms had returned. He looked anxiously at the two newcomers and slowly retreated backward up the alley.

"Victor, we know where to find you." Yin said. "What is Gravicus after?"

"Tell them, and you're a dead man," Gravicus growled.

Yin drew his sword. "Victor, I can be so much more painful."

"The kasilite medallion," the nervous man blurted, then turned and bolted up the alley.

Quinlan was becoming aware that his peril was far from over. He stood between one Shadow Warrior and two other warriors who seemed just as dark, though he wasn't yet sure.

"The kasilite medallion?" the warrior said with delight. At that, his accomplice drew his sword. "That would certainly give us an advantage, now wouldn't it?"

"I found it, and I will take it to Lucius," said Gravicus. "It will restore me to his service!"

The other warrior laughed. "Nothing will restore you, Gravicus.

You have failed him too many times. Now look at you, scuttling about with worthless scum like Victor. You *are* desperate, aren't you?"

Quinlan now realized fully what was happening. The crystal coin was precious indeed, apparently as much to the Shadow Warriors as to anyone else. It was a window into the world of warriors—a tool to expose the secrecy of those dark foes who came from the Kingdom Across the Sea after the rebellion against the King. He considered throwing the crystal coin, or medallion, and making a run for it, but the Shadow Warrior named Yin had said it would give them an advantage.

Could it also identify Silent Warriors? Quinlan wondered. If so, giving up the medallion would be a cowardly and costly action, another event to regret forever. But how could he avoid giving it? He was trapped.

Quinlan glanced from left to right, trying to keep out of sword's reach of all three warriors. The situation seemed hopeless. He readied his sword and slowly backed up toward one side of the alley, where the brick wall of a candle maker's shop offered at least one angle of protection.

"How about this?" Yin offered. "Whoever kills him first gets the medallion."

Both warriors looked at Quinlan with bloodlust in their eyes.

"I have a better idea," a deep voice boomed from across the alleyway.

A narrow passageway between two shops had given access to another warrior. Everyone's attention turned to the newcomer. The tall, muscular figure stood with his hands at his sides, poised and ready for action. Two swords were suspended across his back, crisscrossed so that the hilts were easily accessible.

"Why don't you"—the new warrior pointed to Gravicus—"and you"—he pointed to Yin and his accomplice—"slowly back away from him, and you may live to fight another day…or you can die now."

"You!" Yin spewed. He and his accomplice abandoned their advance on Quinlan and rushed upon the newcomer.

In an instant the warrior had drawn both swords and engaged both Shadow Warriors in a blur of steel. Quinlan had never seen anything like it before. The warrior's mastery was incomprehensible, but Quinlan quickly realized he had a fight of his own. Gravicus had used the distraction of the newcomer's fight with Yin and his companion to attack Quinlan, obviously hoping to win the kasilite medallion for himself. Within three ferocious strokes he had pinned Quinlan up against the brick wall and was recoiling for a final thrust.

"Fight for the Prince, not for yourself!" the newcomer yelled as he parried a thrust and brought a powerful cut across Yin's left shoulder.

Quinlan found strength and hope in his words, for he now realized he was fighting alongside one of the King's own Silent Warriors.

The tip of Gravicus's blade plunged toward his abdomen. Quinlan brought his sword down and across to deflect it at the final moment, and the blade only grazed Quinlan's right thigh. Quinlan's quick backward diagonal cut up sliced across the Shadow Warrior's face, adding one more mark to his plethora of scars. The warrior screamed and pulled back. Fury raged in his eyes as he covered the gash with his left hand.

Quinlan heard another yell as he watched the Silent Warrior withdraw his blade from the chest of Yin's accomplice. The warrior collapsed, and Yin lost heart for the fight. He slowly backed away from his double-bladed opponent and reached for the reins of his horse. When Gravicus saw he would have to face Quinlan and the Silent Warrior alone, he too backed away to a safe distance before turning to run. Yin mounted, rode to the end of the alleyway, and disappeared.

Quinlan leaned against the brick wall, gasping for breath. The Silent Warrior took a moment to scan all directions, then swirled his swords and sheathed both into their scabbards at the same time.

He walked toward Quinlan with large, powerful steps. He was a chiseled weapon of war, and Quinlan imagined he was one of the best. Dark brown hair hung to his neck and framed a clean, handsome face with unnaturally pale gray eyes that compelled Quinlan to look at them.

The warrior glanced down at Quinlan's bleeding thigh, then held out his hand. "Give me the medallion," he commanded.

Quinlan reached into his doublet pocket and withdrew the medallion. He lifted the clear crystal to his eyes and looked through it at the

Silent Warrior. Brilliant violet light emanated from the warrior as if his skin were a brightly lit lantern.

Quinlan slowly put the piece over the warrior's hand to drop it there, but stopped. He looked at the medallion and the broad muscular hand that waited for it, and he pulled back his hand without releasing the crystal coin.

He looked up at the warrior without lifting his head. "How do I know you serve the King?"

The warrior glared at Quinlan as if he might tear him apart and take it anyway. "I fought to save you. Isn't that enough?"

"Those three Shadow Warriors would have done the same if it would get them the medallion."

The warrior took in a great breath, as if willing himself to be patient. "What color did you just see?"

"Violet."

"And when you saw the Shadow Warrior?"

"Green."

"There's your proof," the warrior said. "Now give it to me."

Quinlan still hesitated. The warrior drew himself to full height and crossed his arms across his chest.

"If the medallion falls into the hands of Lucius, his ability to thwart our missions would increase greatly. It would give our enemy a great tactical advantage in this war. Therefore it must be carried by someone who has the skills to protect it."

Quinlan fingered the medallion and ran his thumb over the center crystal. He looked squarely up into the warrior's eyes.

"Can you train me so that I might one day carry it?" he asked.

"No," the warrior replied bluntly.

Quinlan lowered his gaze to the ground.

"I cannot train someone who insists on wallowing in self-pity," the warrior added.

Those words of truth hit Quinlan like a hammer. He realized his pain over the loss of Baylor had indeed moved beyond grief and into self-pity. It was why he stayed so long in Burkfield and why he was now rambling through the kingdom without purpose. He looked back into the gray eyes that had seen a hundred battles.

"Forgive me."

"That is not something I have the power to do," the Silent Warrior said. "Only the Prince can do that."

Quinlan slowly nodded.

"When you are ready, I may come for you." The warrior turned and began to walk away.

Hopelessness pressed in on Quinlan as he watched the warrior go. Part of him wanted to disappear once more into anonymity, but something told him that if he let this moment go, he would forever be a prisoner of his unfulfilled life. He would never escape from being Twitch.

"I am ready now." He took two steps to follow the warrior. "Train me...please."

The warrior stopped and looked over his shoulder.

"You don't know what you're asking for."

"Perhaps. But I can't live like this, denying what I know to live in a kingdom that's destroying itself. I think I would rather die."

The warrior turned. The ferocity of his countenance diminished, though his eyes still burned.

"And die you may," he said softly. "The training I begin is impossible to stop. If you follow me, there is no turning back."

Quinlan considered his words, realizing that Silent Warriors did not have the luxury of exaggeration. He lifted his head, set his shoulders straight, and met the warrior's gaze.

Without a word exchanged, the warrior accepted Quinlan's vow.

"So shall it be. Follow me."

"What is your name, sir?" Quinlan asked as they made their way to the end of the alley.

"My name is Taras."

So this was Baylor's contact. Was his appearance a coincidence? Quinlan followed Taras through the back ways of the city until they reached the countryside.

"But what of my horse and pack?" Quinlan asked.

"They will be recovered. Your steed will be trained as well." Taras picked up the pace. "We will travel on foot to our destination."

"It's not far then?" Quinlan asked.

Taras shook his head. "Chesney Isle lies due west of the Wasteland."

Quinlan stopped in his tracks. The warrior neither stopped nor slowed to wait for him. Quinlan shook himself and sprinted until he was once again traveling beside Taras.

"That's a two-week ride...with a horse!" Quinlan said, breathing hard.

"Mastery of any skill is not to be hurried," Taras replied. "And you have many skills to master. I will take you as far as the Tara Hills. You must make the rest of the journey on your own."

"I have no pack or supplies, only my sword and dagger. How will I—"

"The training begins now, with what you have—nothing more," Taras said a little sharply.

Quinlan had no answer to that. He tried to settle into a rhythm to keep up, but just staying close to Taras required every bit of energy he had. After an hour, Taras stopped to give Quinlan a chance to catch his breath. Quinlan found a tree to lean against.

"How does...," Quinlan asked between gasps, "the kasilite...crystal work?"

Taras seemed hesitant to answer at first. "All of the King's warriors, including the Shadow Warriors before the rebellion, partook of the Life Spice in the Kingdom Across the Sea for many years. Kasilite is an extremely rare crystal that grows only along the shores of the crystal sea near the King's palace. It allows one to see the radiation of the Life Spice emanating from the bodies of those who have ingested it. Shadow Warriors have been without the Life Spice for so long that it is fading within them, causing the light to shift from violet to green and eventually to black."

"Are there other kasilite medallions?" Quinlan asked.

"Not that I'm aware of," Taras replied. "The one you have is unique, crafted by the Prince himself specifically for the Swords of Valor. We thought the Shadow Warriors had taken it from Sir Baylor. It is a great relief to know Lucius does not have it."

Quinlan now understood why Baylor had been so intent on making sure the crystal didn't fall into Shadow Warrior hands. He reached for the medallion and gazed at it, at last fully appreciating the beauty and the power that it represented.

He held it out for Taras to take. "It was meant for the commander of the Swords of Valor...not for me."

Taras reached out and took it from him. "Lesson one—know who you are."

Quinlan took another deep breath and felt like he was almost ready to move on. "What's lesson two?"

Taras looked at him. "Know who you want to become."

THIRTEEN

BECOMING

Quinlan traveled with Taras for many days. They skirted the Vale of the Dragons and crossed the western edge of the Banteen Desert into the region of Nyland. They crossed the western portion of the Red Canyon where its river spills into the Great Sea, then traveled north across the great plains until they reached the foothills of the Tara Hills mountain range.

Throughout the long journey, Taras was careful to avoid all contact with civilization. Quinlan had been raised to hunt and fish, so living off the land was easy for him, but Taras was teaching much more than mere survival. He began instructing Quinlan in the ways of the Silent Warriors, honed over many centuries—how to hide, discover, attack, and disappear, and how to strengthen the body by tearing it down, then building it back up.

In the first two weeks, Quinlan wondered if he could physically endure the grueling regimen Taras set for him, but he did not complain. He forced himself to rise each day despite the screaming protests of his mind and muscles. At night, Taras taught him the lessons of weaponry—especially of the sword—and Quinlan was awestruck by his tutor's mastery.

By the fourth week, Quinlan had begun to feel the benefits of the extreme physical conditioning, and his skill with the sword had improved drastically. Then Taras took him to the next level and pushed him further. Quinlan focused on the fruit of his earlier pain to find the encouragement to keep going. His body grew stronger every day, and though his physique would never match that of Drake or Kessler, Quinlan reveled in his new sense of mastery.

One early morning after six weeks of travel and training, Quinlan stood on a knoll beside Taras, gazing up at the western face of the majestic Tara Hills. This close to the massive towers of rock, soil, and trees, they would not see the sun for several hours.

Taras scrutinized the mountain range and seemed deep in thought.

"What is it, Taras?" Quinlan asked. "What is on your mind?"

In spite of spending every moment of the last six weeks with this Silent Warrior, Quinlan could not say that he knew Taras well. The warrior was guarded in his ways and not given to explanation.

Taras dropped his gaze from the mountains. "Now your training begins."

Quinlan smiled, but Taras did not.

"Begins?" Quinlan asked.

"Yes. These past weeks you have been transitioning into the world of warriors. Without the preparatory conditioning and training you would die within the first day of living here. Now you are ready to learn. If you survive your time in these hills and are able to reenter the world of men, you will know how to help them as a knight *and* as a warrior."

Quinlan's heart sank at Taras's words. He had thought he'd endured the worst part of his training, but now there was much more to come. It was a shock for him to realize how weak and protected he had been his whole life. This kingdom was a hard place, and the ways of it even harder. Every step he took toward understanding that truth took him further and further away from his comfortable life in Burkfield, and he realized he could never go back, not even if he wanted to. It would be like trying to unlearn how to ride a horse. This was a one-way journey.

Taras reached into a pocket and removed the crystal coin Quinlan had given him six weeks earlier. He handed it to Quinlan.

"You will need it in this world." He pointed to a peaceful-looking valley not far away, in the shadows of the mountain range. "Look there."

Quinlan slowly brought the crystal coin up to his eye and looked through it. By holding it at different distances he found he could cause the image to shrink or magnify. He looked toward the valley Taras pointed to, and the air nearly left his lungs. The entire valley glowed a faint green, and many hundreds of individual green glimmers showed in the hills surrounding the valley.

He swallowed hard and fought the fear that swelled within him. He quickly scanned other regions of the mountain and then the plains to the west. Every so often he caught both individual green glimmers and clusters of them. To see farther, he held the crystal coin further away from him, but the image became too blurry to discern anything.

He slowly lowered the crystal coin and stared back at the seemingly peaceful valley. He had just seen what was not supposed to be seen by Arrethtraen eyes, and it shook him.

Is the entire kingdom like this? he wondered.

Quinlan stood in silence, trying to decide if he really wanted to be part of this terrifying world, then realized that everyone in the kingdom already was—they just didn't know it.

"You didn't look through the crystal? How did you know they were there?" he asked Taras.

"I cannot see as clearly as you can through the crystal, but I have learned to see my enemy just the same." Taras finally broke his gaze from the valley and looked at Quinlan. "It is a matter of survival."

"I don't think I can—"

"Remember lesson two—know who you want to become," Taras interrupted. "The Prince sees you not for who you think you are, but for who He knows you are. The truth is that when He died for you on that tree long ago and when you accepted Him as the Son of the King, you already became that which you hope you will become."

"I don't understand," Quinlan said. Taras's words seemed like a convoluted riddle.

Taras took a deep breath, apparently frustrated at trying to explain the significant to the simple.

"Who are you?" he asked.

Quinlan hesitated, confused by the question. "I am Quinlan of Burkfield."

"No!" Taras's eyes glowered. "You are a Knight of the Prince—royal son of the King, heir to the kingdom of Arrethtrae and beyond!"

Taras paced in agitation as he continued. "I and my brothers live and die in service to the King, protecting the Knights of the Prince from the plots and deceptions of Lucius, and yet most of the knights don't even understand who they are in the Prince. We will never be what you already are!"

Quinlan looked up at the mighty warrior in fearful wonder, unnerved by the depth of Taras's emotion. And Taras was not through. "When you believe the truth about who you are in the Prince," he said, "you will be that which you want to become. You cannot add anything to that which the Prince made perfect. All you can do is believe Him who made it so. Then and only then will you be ready."

"Ready for what?" Quinlan asked.

"The Swords of Valor. They need you."

Quinlan froze, stared, then finally shook his head. "I'll never be the knight that Kessler, Drake, or Purcell is."

"I trained Baylor," Taras said bluntly. "I can train you."

"I am no Baylor," Quinlan retorted. "And I never will be."

"You're not supposed to be," Taras replied angrily. "You're supposed to be Quinlan." He strode to the far edge of the knoll.

"Where are you going?"

"Over here, so I don't strike you," Taras replied with his back to Quinlan.

Quinlan's eyes widened, and he stayed silent. Evidently even a Silent Warrior could be pushed too far, and Taras was closer to the edge than Quinlan had realized.

After a few moments Taras walked back across the knoll. He stared at Quinlan for a long while.

"I'm sorry, Taras," Quinlan said, "but the thought of my becoming a true knight of the Swords of Valor seems…far-fetched. Kessler, Drake, and Purcell would never fight with me now. If that is what this is for, then—"

"You were chosen for this training, Quinlan."

Quinlan was confused until he realized his meeting with Taras had not been a coincidence after all.

"Why?" he asked. "Kessler, Drake, or Purcell would do so much better with your training. Why not choose one of them?"

"I do not choose. The Prince chooses."

Quinlan looked at Taras in disbelief, then turned away, overwhelmed by the thought.

"Besides," Taras said, "the others cannot see through the crystal as you do."

Quinlan recovered himself and turned back to Taras, a question on his face. "Not everyone can see the glowing green and violet?"

"No. Only those chosen by the Prince. Do you remember the fire that killed your parents?"

Quinlan nodded, wondering what that long-ago tragedy had to do with the crystal coin.

"Do you remember how the smoke and heat burned in your eyes?" Taras continued.

"Yes." Quinlan winced at the painful memory. "When I awoke that night, the fire was raging everywhere. I screamed for my mother and father, but…it was already too late. The heat and the smoke were so intense I knew I was going to die. I could hardly see—everything was a blur, and my eyes hurt so much. A man carried me out of our house and set me beside a tree. He rubbed some kind of ointment into my eyes. I started to scream, but he told me to be calm. Slowly the pain diminished, but I couldn't see anything. I thought I'd gone blind."

Quinlan closed his eyes. "Others came and tried to save my parents, but the house collapsed. When they came to me and washed my eyes, everything was still blurry, but the pain was gone. Then, over the next few days, I began to see clearly again."

"Who was the man that saved you?" Taras asked.

Quinlan shook his head. "I don't know." He looked up at Taras. "Was it—"

"The Prince knows how to use the catastrophes of our lives to make something good. That is why you can see warriors through the crystal coin. Many people have such gifts, but until they yield to the King's call-ing, they will never know it. The day you knelt on Mount Resolute and swore your complete allegiance to the Prince was the day that put the rest of your life in motion. The Prince had been waiting for you all these years."

Quinlan's brow furrowed. "But Sir Baylor came for Tav."

"Sir Baylor *assumed* he came for Tav because of his skills, but in truth I sent him for the one who was willing to give all to the Prince."

Taras looked as though he was preparing to start the day's journey. "In time, and if you complete the training, you won't even need the crys-tal coin to see the enemy. The Prince gave to you what is in the coin. You just don't believe it yet."

I believe, my Prince, Quinlan said within himself. *Please help me when I don't believe.*

Quinlan lifted the crystal coin to his eye once more and gazed at the luminescent valley.

"So many evil hearts in one place," he said in a hushed tone. "What are they doing there?" he asked as he lowered the crystal coin…but Taras was not there.

The hairs on Quinlan's neck stood straight. He instinctively dropped to the ground, then crawled to the cover of a small tree. A twig snapped to his left, followed by silence. His heart began to race. Though the valley was a fair distance away, he had seen green glimmers all over. Surely they were in this area too.

He peered through the crystal and saw two glowing green figures perhaps fifty paces away, coming closer. He scanned farther until he saw the slightest hint of violet light emanating from the undergrowth on the far side of the knoll.

He returned the coin to his pocket and carefully drew his sword, hoping they hadn't spotted him. He didn't feel ready to face a Shadow Warrior one on one yet. He quietly retreated to heavier vegetation and slid his bright sword beneath the pine needles and soft soil as Taras had taught him. He soiled his face with the black dirt of the forest floor to dull the shine of his pale skin, then grabbed the hilt of his sword and listened. He could just see their approach out of the corner of his eyes.

"I'm tired of patrolling this forsaken mountain," one of the Shadow Warriors said.

The two warriors walked close to the spot where Taras and Quinlan had just been standing, and stopped. The first warrior held up his hand to shush his comrade and knelt down. Quinlan's heart was now beating so loudly he was sure the warriors could hear it. He held his breath, gripped his sword tightly, and waited.

"What is it?" the standing warrior asked.

The other warrior looked all around, then stood. "Nothing. Let's go."

The two warriors proceeded on, and Quinlan started to breathe again. He waited to move until he saw Taras stand and then quietly joined him.

"They didn't see us," Quinlan whispered.

"Perhaps not." Taras kept his eyes in the direction the warriors had gone. "But they know we are here."

"How could you tell?" Quinlan asked.

"That was Baraat." Taras scowled. "He doesn't miss anything. He just didn't know how many of us there are and considered the risk too great to give alarm. But he will report our presence, and now your mission will be all the more difficult."

"What mission?"

"Discover why that valley is glowing so green."

FOURTEEN

CLOSE TO THE ENEMY

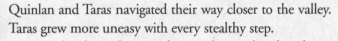

Quinlan and Taras navigated their way closer to the valley. Taras grew more uneasy with every stealthy step.

Quinlan kept the crystal coin close at hand and was able to help them avoid multiple patrols. As the sun rose higher into the sky and the western face of the mountain became brighter, however, his range of identification lessened, so he and Taras staggered their advance. One would serve as lookout while the other moved ahead and found cover.

They had just evaded a group of three Shadow Warriors near the rim of the small valley when two more mounted warriors appeared. "Lord Hatlin," one of the newcomers said, "the patrols are reporting all clear."

The warrior named Hatlin glared at his subordinate, then slowly scanned the area himself. The mere sight of him made Quinlan shudder. He was a massive figure who wore a constant scowl, creased by decades of evil deeds. Quinlan imagined his face was but a faint image of the darkened mind and heart behind it. His silver armor fit his muscular torso snugly and was ornately decked with gold and red markings that apparently signified his position and allegiance. The other four warriors, though intimidating, seemed inferior in every way.

"Widen the patrols," Hatlin commanded. "Lord Luskan makes his report to Master Lucius tomorrow, and I don't want to tell him we've been compromised."

"Yes, my lord." The reporting warrior galloped off with his comrade, clearly anxious to be out of Hatlin's presence. Hatlin sat still on his mount for another moment while the other two warriors waited tensely.

"I smell something, Ectar." Hatlin turned to his lieutenant. "I'm holding you personally responsible for security within the inner ring. Do you understand?"

The warrior named Ectar saluted. "Yes, my lord."

"Get the warriors you need. I brief Lord Luskan this afternoon. Notify me immediately if you discover anything." Hatlin pulled on the reins of his horse and wheeled around.

"Even if it means interrupting your briefing?" Ectar asked.

"Of course, you imbecile!" Hatlin kicked his horse, who reared and bolted off in the direction from which they'd come.

Ectar scowled after Hatlin, then turned on the remaining warrior. "Don't sit there gawking, dolt. Fetch me thirty warriors immediately!"

Quinlan and Taras waited until both warriors had left; then Taras crawled the short distance to Quinlan. A look of grave concern was on his face.

"How many warriors did you see through the crystal earlier?" he whispered.

"I'm not sure," Quinlan replied. "Perhaps a thousand."

Taras's eyes widened. "We need to get out of here now!"

"What's happening?" Quinlan asked.

"Had I known how many there are—or *who* they are—I would have never risked this." Taras clenched his jaw. "Luskan and Hatlin are Lucius's top two commanders. Whatever is happening here is serious— *very* serious."

He looked for the best cover for their retreat and pointed. "We'll travel northeast and give a wide berth to this valley. Once we're clear, you must travel to Chesney Isle just off the coast in the north country, due west of the Wasteland. A Silent Warrior named Rafe will continue your training in my absence. Here, you'll need this."

Taras handed Quinlan a vellum map of the kingdom, and Quinlan stuffed it into his tunic. "Where are you going?" he asked, a little disconcerted.

"I must report our findings to headquarters. If we get separated"—Taras hesitated, apparently contemplating his own words—"you must continue your travel north as planned."

Quinlan nodded, though the idea of navigating in this hostile country without Taras seemed unthinkable.

Moving slowly and carefully, Taras led the first leg out away from the valley. Quinlan looked through the crystal coin for some sign of the enemy while he waited for Taras to find cover. Taras was perhaps fifty paces northeast when he signaled for Quinlan to come, but just as Quinlan began to move, he heard a horse snort. He ducked back into his hiding place and looked through the coin again. An entire contingent of mounted Shadow Warriors was coming his way.

Quinlan pressed himself into a thicket of heavy brush, then peered out to see thirteen warriors halted right between him and Taras. He recognized the one named Ectar, who ordered, "Set your posts up along this line within sight of each other across the valley rim. Any breach of this inner circle, and I will personally see to your lashings."

Ectar slapped his steed and rode off. Two of the remaining warriors dismounted and separated, remaining just within visual range of each other, which was not far considering the thick foliage of the area. The other ten split and rode farther left and right to set up their posts.

Quinlan tried to stay calm as he considered his options. Evidently he was already in the inner circle of the Shadow Warrior patrols, and Taras had just crossed outside of it. There was no way they could reconnect without being identified. Quinlan doubted he could even move without being spotted.

He stayed perfectly still for a long while, waiting for the Shadow Warriors to become bored at their posts. Fortunately, as the day warmed, the wind began to blow. The forest trees rustled and creaked, affording him a sound cover from which to attempt a move.

The two nearest guards were still directly between him and Taras.

Inch by inch, timing each painfully slow movement with the sounds of the wind, Quinlan was able to move away from them, down into the valley below. He was traveling the wrong direction, but he had no choice. He hoped to find a better location to breach the inner circle of patrols, but the farther he crawled, the more impossible that seemed. As he continued inward toward the base camp, however, he noticed that the security actually decreased. Presumably the camp patrols had been pulled out to the inner circle.

At that point, Quinlan conceived a bold yet potentially foolish idea. He was already trapped, so why not learn as much as possible? Taras needed to report the situation, but they still didn't know what it was really all about. If Quinlan could get close enough to actually hear something of importance, the information could be invaluable.

Quinlan tried to implement every detail of Taras's training as he maneuvered closer and closer to the heart of the Shadow Warrior camp. The crystal coin saved him twice and helped him avoid a dozen other encounters.

He finally stopped at a shallow ridge line to collect himself. He knew that being discovered would mean instant death, and he was amazed that the timid Twitch of Burkfield was even considering his next action. He knew he dared not hesitate long. Given enough time, his fear of entering one of the darkest abodes of evil would overcome the courage that drove him onward.

The ridge line gave him the first view of the camp below. It was hardly a camp at all, just a single, heavily guarded tent, but everything about the place whispered secrecy.

Quinlan cut leafy branches from shrubs and tied the stems to his arms, legs, and back. Then he slowly moved closer, crawling the last one hundred paces to the outskirts of the camp. The near side of the tent was less heavily guarded, but Quinlan still had a difficult time getting close enough to hear anything.

Using painstakingly slow moves, he finally maneuvered to within a few paces of the tent. He sank into a natural recess near a group of trees, covered himself in pine needles, dirt, and brush, and waited.

He heard insignificant chatter among some of the warriors within and an occasional order by a warrior he thought was Hatlin. But after two hours of fruitless waiting, he wondered if he had risked his life for nothing. By now the sun was well along on its journey to the western horizon, and Quinlan began to think about retreating from the camp to prepare for an escape at nightfall. Just as he was preparing to move, however, he heard a flurry of activity in the camp.

"Commander approaching," a warrior called out. A minute later, Quinlan heard the hoofbeats of many heavy horses. From his vantage point, he could only get a brief glimpse of the arriving warriors but could tell that their leader was as formidable as Hatlin, if not more so, with cropped black hair, piercing eyes, and a long, arrogant-looking nose. This commander dismounted and handed his reins to a subordinate, then took a moment to scan the camp.

Quinlan's heart skipped a beat as the commander's gaze swept over his hiding place and seemed to pause. How far did the powers of this dark warrior go?

"I trust you received my men this morning and secured the area?" Quinlan went limp with relief as the commander turned to address Hatlin.

"Yes, Lord Luskan. Each of the region lords have also reported in. How is Master Lucius?"

"He is impatient with our progress. Come, let's begin." Luskan ducked into the tent. Hatlin and four other warriors followed.

A lamp flared in the tent, allowing Quinlan to make out shadowy figures gathered about a table. The warriors bent over to look at what Quinlan assumed was a map.

"Give me a full situation report on each of the regions and their major cities," Luskan commanded.

"In the southwest, Daydelon is proving to be an excellent location from which to launch our chaos attacks on Chessington. Lord Malizimar is challenged in uniting the Vinceros toward a common cause, but we believe he is making progress. Al Kirut is another city that is…"

Quinlan's heart became heavy as he listened to Hatlin's report and realized the impact the Shadow Warriors were having from one end of the kingdom to the other. The sleeping masses of the people had no idea these dark warriors were discussing their future demise.

"Master Lucius is eager for the Rising, but every region and their major cities must be under our control," Luskan said. "What of the Camerians?"

There was a delay in Hatlin's answer. "Well?" Luskan demanded.

"The Knights of the Prince there are still strong. We are working on them, but it is proving to be a challenge. Why not just isolate them and proceed with the Rising?"

"Because they are one of the strongest regions in the kingdom, and they will continue to support the King's people in Chessington."

The commander's shadow, projected on the tent walls, paced back and forth. "This is unacceptable, and Master Lucius will not be pleased!" He stopped and slammed his fist on the table. "Get control of Cameria, or you and I will be sent there personally to oversee the operation. Is that clear?"

"Yes...Commander." Quinlan sensed the slightest edge of insolence in Hatlin's answer, and he wondered if there wasn't a measure of contention between the two Shadow Warriors.

"Now, how goes Master Lucius's project at Burkfield?" Luskan asked. "Has Pathyon made a fool of himself yet?"

Quinlan felt shivers run up and down his spine at the mention of his home city. He hung on every word.

"Do not be so quick to judge Lord Pathyon, Commander. With minimal resources and in short order, he has gained nearly complete control of the city and effectively incapacitated the Knights of the Prince there."

"So it *is* true." Luskan turned away from the table and paced again. "How many Vincero Knights has he employed?"

"None," Hatlin replied. "I think that's why the Knights of the Prince were caught off guard."

"It's a fluke. That weasel couldn't conquer a village, let alone a city the size of Burkfield."

"Perhaps," Hatlin said. "But evidently Master Lucius thinks more highly of him than you do, and thus far he's been right."

Luskan froze, then whirled about. "Are you mocking me, Lord Hatlin?"

Quinlan saw the four other warriors slowly step back as their leaders faced off. He felt the immense tension even from his camouflaged hideaway. After a long period of silence, Hatlin spoke.

"Of course not, Commander Luskan. I'm only suggesting we may have something to learn from the tactics Lord Pathyon has employed at Burkfield. Perhaps a variation of his strategy could be used against the United Cities of Cameria."

Luskan hesitated with his hand on his dagger. "Ha," he snorted, "I suppose it is something we'll have to consider. For now, though, we will continue to carry out Master Lucius's plan for Burkfield. Its destruction will be an example for the rest of the Knights of the Prince to see. Show me where our warriors are positioned."

"Here and here." The tension abated as the two warriors returned their full attention to the map. "Do we move now?" Hatlin asked.

"No. Lucius wants to draw more citizens and knights into the trap. I suspect he'll want Burkfield's destruction to occur closer to the Rising. Send two companies of warriors to ensure that Pathyon doesn't lose what he's gained. I can guarantee the Silent Warriors are working with the Knights of the Prince to break his stronghold there. If there is even the slightest shift in our domination, I want to know immediately."

"Of course," Hatlin replied. "What of Taras and the Swords of Valor? Can we expect any engagements?"

"After Baylor's death, they completely disbanded." Luskan sounded pleased. "My assassination squad is watching them closely, however. The Prince can't protect them forever."

At that, all six warriors stood straight.

"The time is coming, and the Rising is near, comrades," Luskan proclaimed. "We will crush the heads of His knights with an iron boot and rule Arrethtrae beside Lucius forever."

The warriors all placed fisted hands to their chests.

"Praise Lucius!" Luskan shouted.

"Praise Lucius!" the other five warriors echoed.

Quinlan shuddered, repulsed and frightened by the sound of that evil acclamation. He had heard enough, but now he faced the dilemma of how to escape with his information—and his life.

He decided to wait until evening, when the crystal coin would offer him the best detection. While he waited, thoughts and questions raced through his head: Cameria…Assassins…Baylor…the Rising, whatever that was.

Of it all, however, the one that occupied his mind the most was home…Burkfield.

FIFTEEN

LILAM OF NOREX

As darkness fell, Quinlan slowly made his way back up the valley. Though his stomach howled in hunger, he did not allow a single move to be rushed. Though the odds of his safe exodus were slim, he kept reminding himself that every minute he wasn't discovered was one minute closer to escape.

The crystal coin saved his life time and time again. To see and not be seen gave him a great tactical advantage. He kept looking for the violet light of a Silent Warrior, hoping to find Taras, but he could only see as far as the thick trees allowed.

Travel through the black of night was excruciatingly slow, but by early morning, Quinlan had made it to the rim of the valley to discover the security detail had been terminated. He was still extremely careful as he made his way far beyond the valley.

Only when there were no glimmers of green within any line of sight did he finally allow himself to relax. Then fatigue rushed in like a flood. He fed on a handful of blackberries and wild onions before lying down in a well-camouflaged grassy bed.

Quinlan slept until midafternoon, then resumed his journey north along the foothills of the mountain range. Travel proved far more diffi-cult on his own, but Taras had taught him well, and he continued in the world of warriors. He made his way through the Plains of Kerr and into the southern fringes of the north country. The flat countryside was sparsely populated and broadly scattered with farms and ranches that raised cattle, goats, and sheep. Clusters of trees afforded a pleasant break from the green and golden fields that stretched from horizon to horizon.

After twenty days of traveling, Quinlan approached the city of Norwex. Standing on a hill still some distance away, he looked down on the city and considered stopping to resupply for the next leg of the journey. A bed and warm meal held a strong appeal, but he hesitated since Taras had implied he was to avoid all people. Finally Quinlan decided to circumnavigate Norwex and press on to Chesney Isle.

He set a course east of the city that took him through a large grove of trees. As he emerged from their shadows, he heard voices and the sounds of a ruckus.

Before him was a stone-rimmed well surrounded by agitated sheep and goats. Several low stone retaining walls led up near the well, where two shepherds were facing off. What really caught his attention was the fact that one of them was a teenage girl and the other was a brute half again as big as she.

"You know full well this is my father's land and his well." The young woman positioned herself firmly between the man and the water source.

"Not today it's not," the man said with a sneer. "I say it's ours, so move your sheep aside for our goats before I begin slicing them open."

The man stepped forward, grabbed the girl by the shoulders, and was about to throw her out of the way, but she moved so quickly that Quinlan's mouth fell open in awe. She wrapped her right arm around the man's left forearm, then fell to one knee while simultaneously rotating her body, pulling the man forward and down over her firmly planted right leg. The man lurched forward and fell face first onto the ground. Quinlan stifled a laugh, but then he spotted two other men approaching from the direction of the goats.

"Letting a girl get the best of you, Yelton? Father will be so proud!"

The badgering enraged the embarrassed brute further. He jumped to his feet and drew a sword. "You'll pay for that, wench."

The girl didn't hesitate. She ran to a nearby retaining wall, dove over it, and appeared an instant later with a sword unlike any Quinlan had ever seen. It was as long as a typical sword, but the blade was slightly curved and a bit narrower. She placed a hand on the wall and leaped over it with the agility of a cat.

"Now, this ought to be fun," one of the approaching men said.

Quinlan maneuvered along one of the retaining walls to position himself behind the men as the fight began. He wanted to be ready…just in case.

The two engaged, and within the first few cuts, Quinlan could tell that the girl was twice the swordsman the man was. Twice she parried and countered with a cut that would have severely wounded the man, but she pulled up short each time. Quinlan was impressed, to say the least.

At one point she caught the man's vertical slice, then countered and thrust just as one of the other men pushed her from behind with his boot. She lurched forward into her opponent and her sword sliced through his left arm.

The fight paused as blood ran down the man's arm and dripped onto the ground. He looked up with fury in his eyes.

"She cut me!" he screamed. "You're gonna regret that, wench!"

The man attacked with a vengeance, but the girl held her ground. The other two men, whom Quinlan now assumed were his brothers, looked at each other and nodded. They drew their swords and raised them to strike the girl from the back.

"Now that doesn't seem quite fair." Quinlan leaped over the stone wall behind the two men. They turned in time to see him draw his sword.

Both men turned on Quinlan with a rash volley of cuts. To his surprise, he easily handled both at the same time until they spread apart and divided his attention. He worked his way toward the girl to cover her back and afford some protection for himself as well. The two of them fought back to back, frustrating the angry trio of brothers.

Not sure how long the girl could keep her brute at bay, Quinlan thrust at what appeared to be the oldest brother to put him in retreat, then made two powerful cuts on the other, followed by a thrust and a binding move Taras had taught him. The man's sword flew from his hand, and Quinlan turned to the older brother before it hit the ground. He advanced so quickly that the man stumbled backward and fell. Quinlan quickly set the tip of his sword at the man's throat.

"Drop your swords," he commanded.

The man on the ground dropped his sword, but Quinlan could hear the girl still locked in a deadly duel. Quinlan pressed his sword into the prone man's throat. "Yelton!" the man hollered.

The twang of swords ceased.

"But she cut me!" Yelton gasped, clearly winded by the fight.

"Drop it, you oaf!" the man on the ground yelled.

When Quinlan heard the sword hit the ground, he withdrew and turned to face the others.

"Get your animals off her land," he ordered.

The injured man clamped his right hand on his wound and joined his two brothers. The three of them began separating the goats from the sheep and moving them away from the well.

"I could have handled them myself," the girl said. She'd come to stand beside Quinlan. He looked over to see confident hazel eyes staring at him. She tossed her head to flick black hair from her square shoulders. She looked a few years younger than Quinlan but was nearly as tall.

Quinlan hid a smile. "Yes. I could see that."

"Thanks just the same," the girl said.

Quinlan nodded. "You handle that sword very well." He looked back toward the men who had just harassed her as he snapped his own sword into its scabbard. "Are you going to be all right?"

"Of course," the girl huffed. "Why wouldn't I be?"

Quinlan raised an eyebrow and shrugged. He was ready to be on his way. He gave her a farewell nod, looked north past Norwex, and started walking, but he'd gone only a few steps when the girl appeared at his right side.

"Hey, where are you from?" she asked, swinging her sword about with the skill of a trained fighter.

"South of here."

"No kidding—you and the rest of the kingdom."

Quinlan shook his head and walked faster.

"If you're a knight, where's your horse?" The girl had to hop a bit to keep pace with Quinlan as he lengthened his stride.

"I didn't say I was a knight," he replied.

"No, but you fight like one and you look like one...mostly." She peered into his face to see if she could get a reaction.

Quinlan smirked, and she smiled.

"I need to be on my way." Quinlan picked up his pace a little more. "You be careful."

She stopped walking. Quinlan felt bad about shooing her off, but he had too far to go and too much to do to get caught up in some quirky north-country feud. He glanced very briefly over his right shoulder to make sure she was gone and breathed a sigh of relief.

"Hey!" The girl's voice jolted him.

Quinlan snapped his head to the left to find her walking briskly beside him. "Don't you have sheep to tend?"

She bolted ahead a couple of steps, jumped in front of him, and held up her hand for him to stop. "Look, I'm really grateful you helped me out back there." Her eyes softened as she turned the flat of her hand on its side to offer it to him.

Quinlan sighed and shook her hand. "You're welcome."

She looked down at his tunic. "You're a Knight of the Prince."

At that, Quinlan stalled. "How do you know about the Knights of the Prince?"

"A knight came through nearly a year ago talking about the Prince." She seemed to gaze through him and into her memory of the event.

"Really?" Quinlan tried not to sound too skeptical. "What do you know of Him?"

"I know that He is the Son of the true King of Arrethtrae and that He came to teach all of the kingdom His ways...whether man or *woman*!"

Quinlan couldn't help grinning at that. Her exuberance was infectious.

"I also know He died for us and the King brought Him back to life through the Life Spice. He's coming back for those who are found faithful. The knight explained it all at a meeting outside of Norwex one evening." The girl glanced toward the city. "I wanted to talk to him, but my father and brothers wouldn't let me. They said it was all nonsense, but I believed it. I've always known we had a good King. The knight's words gave me hope, and I knew I wanted to belong to the King and His Son."

The girl looked at Quinlan with yearning eyes. "I decided that night that I would join the Prince no matter what. Then I met Master Kwi."

The girl smiled, and Quinlan realized the gleam in her eye could come only from one who knew the truth.

"Master Kwi is a Knight of the Prince too?"

"Yes. He came to our region not long after. He knighted me, and I've been training under him ever since." The girl whipped her sword from side to side as if it were an extension of her body.

"It is good to meet a fellow knight this far north. What's your name, miss?" Quinlan asked.

"My name is Lilam. Will you train me further?"

Quinlan balked at that. He didn't feel qualified to teach much of anything to anyone, let alone a girl who already seemed an expert in both sword fighting and hand-to-hand combat.

"It looks to me as though Master Kwi has done a thorough job already," he said. "I should like to meet him sometime."

She held up the sword she'd been carrying and offered the hilt to Quinlan. He grasped the sword and held it before him. Though much lighter than he was used to, it was a comfortable fit.

"The sword belongs to him," Lilam said, "but he wanted me to keep it near so I could practice every day...and I do."

"It shows," Quinlan said. "This is a beautiful weapon."

He drew his own sword and offered it to Lilam. Her eyes drank in every detail. She used it to engage an invisible enemy, and Quinlan was impressed once more by her skill. They swapped swords again, and Lilam looked a bit sad.

"It's what I was born to be." She held up her sword and stared at it, then turned imploring eyes to Quinlan. "Please train me further. I want to learn more so I can fully serve the Prince."

"I—I'm sorry, Lilam. I'm on a special mission and must continue this very day. There is much at stake."

"For the Prince?" she asked.

"Yes."

"Then take me with you. I will help you, and you can train me along the way."

Quinlan stared at her, dumbfounded. "Surely you jest," he said; but Lilam's face was serious. "That just isn't something I can do," he added. "Besides, you have a family here and sheep to tend. You are too young to be on a mission just yet."

Her eyes sparked. "I'll be twenty next month—probably not much younger than you."

She was right, Quinlan realized. She was older than she looked, nearly his own age. He shook his head and rubbed his neck, wondering how to convince her.

"It's impossible, Lilam," he said as gently as possible. "Surely your father would never allow such a thing."

Lilam continued to plead with her eyes. "Before I became a Knight of the Prince, I ached for purpose in my life. Now that I have found it and am called to fight for Him, I'm left to tend sheep. One more day here, and I think I shall—"

"Lilam!" a voice called from near the well where the skirmish occurred.

Lilam turned about and sighed. "I'm here, Father."

A stocky gentleman with salt-and-pepper hair hurried toward them.

"What's going on, Lilam? You're supposed to be bringing the sheep in, and they are scattered all over the place."

"Father, the brothers from Brouwer ranch attacked me and tried to take our well again," Lilam said.

"What?" her father exclaimed. "Are you hurt? I knew I should've sent one of your brothers with you."

Lilam placed her hands firmly on her hips. "I'm fine, but Yelton will be nursing a wound for a while."

Her father shook his head. "I'm not surprised, daughter. But you're lucky they didn't do the same to you."

"They tried, but this gentleman stepped in and sa—*helped* me. Father, please meet Sir—" Lilam turned to Quinlan with a look of embarrassment. "I don't even know your name!"

"Quinlan, sir—pleased to meet you."

The man took Quinlan's hand. "Nelson's my name. I'm indebted to you, sir, for helping my daughter. Will you join us for dinner this evening?"

"Yes," Lilam said with a sly smile. "We insist on showing our gratitude. You simply must come for dinner."

Quinlan glared briefly at Lilam. "I should really be on my—"

Nelson held up his hand. "I insist. You look like you could use a good meal anyway, son." He turned and walked away, apparently expecting Quinlan to follow.

With a sigh, Quinlan gave in, and soon he was helping herd sheep back to a large ranch. "I should have listened to Taras," he muttered to himself as he cleaned up for supper with Lilam and her family.

The meal was beyond superb—roast lamb, fresh greens, boiled potatoes, and baked apples—and the conversation was pleasant and noninvasive. Quinlan learned that Lilam was the third of eight children and that her two older brothers had just gotten back from selling some sheep in the city. He shared a little about his own home and thanked Lilam's mother for a second helping.

Quinlan was surprised how comfortable he felt with the family—until one of the youngest brothers blurted, "Lilam says you're a knight on a mission. Where are you going?"

Quinlan smiled at the lad. "North."

Lilam looked at her father and her brothers.

"How far north?" her oldest brother asked.

Quinlan caught the subtle concern. "Far north," he replied. "To Chesney Isle."

At that, the family stopped eating—all except the nine-month-old. "What takes you up that far north?" Lilam's father asked, breaking the silence.

"I'm not at liberty to say," Quinlan replied. "Is there something I should be concerned about?"

Lilam looked him straight in the eye with grave concern on her face. "If you're going to Chesney Isle, you'll have to pass through the Dunes of Mynar. That's a very treacherous land, especially near the Kang River."

"Why's that?" Quinlan asked.

"First, the land before the river is very dry," she said. "Second"— Lilam hesitated and looked around the table at her family. "some say it is inhabited by sand monsters called penthomoths."

"Penthomoths?" Quinlan didn't care much for monsters. "Are we talking about creatures with long teeth and sharp claws? Poisonous perhaps?"

"No," her older brother replied. "None of that."

"How bad can they be, then?" Quinlan smiled to ease the tension. No one else smiled.

"We don't really know what they look like," Nelson said, "just that when they attack, tentacles come up from the sand and the victim disappears...forever."

"And there are other critters, large and small, along the river that are just as dangerous," Nelson said. "People just avoid that region."

Quinlan swallowed hard. "I appreciate your warning, but I must travel there all the same. I'll keep a sharp eye out." He changed the subject, mostly for his own peace of mind, and before long the pleasantness of the meal was restored.

Quinlan found Lilam's family delightful—so delightful, in fact, that he let himself be talked into spending the night. He drifted off to sleep in a soft bed and only woke up once with tentacles wrapped around his leg, but then they disappeared, and he was once more fast asleep.

SIXTEEN

THE DUNES
OF MYNAR

Quinlan ended up staying three more days with Lilam's family, enjoying a hospitable respite from his journey. Whenever possible during that time, Lilam enticed him to train her further with the sword and to talk of missions for the Prince. Quinlan thoroughly enjoyed himself but decided he'd best move on quickly before he became too comfortable there. Trying to disengage was like trying to remove a bandage from a wound, especially since he had come to know Lilam's heart.

He left her with a promise to return some day and take her to join other Knights of the Prince in the southern half of the kingdom—if, and only if, her father gave his approval. Lilam sadly accepted his terms and allowed him to leave without too much grief.

After leaving the ranch and continuing his journey north, Quinlan gradually settled back into the mind-set of the warrior Taras had started training him to be. He frequently used the crystal coin to search for Shadow Warriors, but since leaving the Tara Hills he had seen none.

After about ten days of travel, Quinlan noticed a significant change in the landscape. The lush green plains gradually gave way to drier, more rugged terrain. Then one day he climbed to the ridge of a jagged hill and looked out over a bleak but strangely beautiful landscape. Starting at the base of the hill and stretching as far as the eye could see was a sea of sand piled up in shifting dunes, interrupted only by the occasional rock towers that jutted hundreds of feet into the air.

The towers varied in shape and diameter. Some were as large as forty to fifty feet across and solid from top to bottom, while others narrowed to just a couple of feet at the base and looked as if they might topple at any moment. In fact, Quinlan could see that a few of the towers had indeed fallen and were slowly being absorbed into the sea of sand below. On the tops and in natural alcoves in the sides of the larger towers sprouted green grass, shrubs, flowers, and even a few small trees— pleasing oases in the otherwise barren land.

Quinlan consulted his map and calculated he was only two or three days away from the coastal area opposite Chesney Isle. He wasn't sure how he would actually reach the island but decided to trust Taras and continue following his instructions. He checked his supplies—conserving water would be an obvious priority—and slid down the hill to the Dunes of Mynar.

Quinlan soon learned that crossing a desert of shifting sand required a completely different manner of travel. At first he felt the sand would swallow him with every step, but he slowly adjusted to the way he had to walk. It was exhausting, though, and his progress was far slower than he had expected. He mentally allowed another day or two to make his destination and settled into observing the region.

A variety of animal life thrived in this strange habitat—lizards, brown snakes, crablike creatures, four or five different species of birds, and a myriad of fast-moving insects. One time he saw a wave of sand moving across the ground when there was no wind to move it. Whatever creature caused that seemed to be a master of subterranean motion.

The massive towers looked to be the cornerstone of life for the dune dwellers, providing both plant life for food and shade from the sun—for even this far north, the sand heated up quickly in the summer sun. Quinlan had to adapt his culinary tastes to his new environment. After learning how to capture and kill the brown snakes, those became his favorite meal.

The nights were chilly and filled with noises that sounded like calls from the throats of strange beasts. Lilam's family's warnings about the sand monsters lingered in his memory, so he made a point to spend each night in a sheltered alcove of one of the towers. As time passed, he was comforted to realize that large sounds often came from small creatures. One sound he couldn't identify, however, was a trumpeted cry comprised of a steady bass pitch and successively higher treble pitches. The effect was quite eerie, especially since he heard it only after sundown.

One day when he was nearly two-thirds of the way through the desert, he traveled too late into the evening and could find no tower with alcoves within his climbing reach. When the light was nearly gone, he was forced to make camp on the sand near the base of a tower. With his dagger in hand and his sword close by, Quinlan tried to rest. The desert noises echoed around him, and sleep was slow to come, but eventually the weariness of the day pulled his eyes shut.

In the middle of the night, Quinlan had the strangest sensation that Tav was pulling on his leg, trying to wake him for the day's work. He reached for the leg, but something held his arm down. Instantly he was jarred out of his sleep and into a nightmare of reality. Multiple snakelike tentacles had wrapped around his legs and arms and were slowly and silently pulling him down into the sand.

Quinlan tried to sit up; his heart was racing. In the dim moonlight, he could see another tentacle swishing around the air above him. He tried to avoid it, but he was pinned and sinking quickly. The tentacle felt for his torso, and he knew it would soon wrap around his neck and strangle him.

Quinlan screamed, but the steady pull on his body continued. He realized he was still clinging to his dagger, but he could not turn the blade far enough to reach the tentacle. His legs were going into the sand first and at an angle. He could no longer see his feet or knees.

He fought with all his might to free one of his arms, but the tentacles only tightened in his resistance. The floating tentacle found his neck and slowly began to curl around his throat. He felt something brush against his knife hand and realized it was yet another tentacle. He rotated his wrist, set the knife's sharp edge against the tentacle, and sliced as deeply as he could.

All at once the tentacles jolted, and he heard a muffled cry below him. The tentacle wrapped around his neck released. So did the one around his knife hand.

Quinlan quickly rotated his body and sliced at the tentacle around his left hand. This time he had the power to cut deep into it. Instantly the pull on his legs stopped, and all of the tentacles released. Quinlan tried to climb out of the sand, but the ground shifted beneath him, and he felt as though he were falling into a funnel. Then, just a few feet away, the sand erupted like a geyser, and the air reverberated with the ear-piercing multitoned trumpet cry.

Quinlan crawled away on his back, but he could not move fast enough. In the faint moonlight Quinlan's imagination filled in the sketchy details of a demon creature of nightmarish proportions. Though it was still partially imbedded in the sand, Quinlan could tell its body was at least as large as a horse, perhaps larger. The tentacles thrashed wildly in front of it. The creature trumpeted again as Quinlan tried desperately to free himself from the collapsing sand. He seemed to be falling closer and closer toward what he knew would be horrible jaws.

Finally Quinlan turned on his stomach and was able to crawl twice as fast. He could just see the glimmer of the moon off the edge of his sword in front of him. His fingers barely touched the hilt just as a tentacle wrapped around his leg. He fully expected a set of massive jaws to clamp down on him at any instant, but instead he was yanked into the air like a rag doll and thrown hard against the nearby rock tower.

The trumpet cry of the creature was the last thing he heard before all went black.

SEVENTEEN

A FRIEND'S RESCUE

Quinlan blinked, but the sun seemed to burn holes in his eyes. His head throbbed, and his mouth was dry as cotton. Starting with his fingers, he slowly moved one appendage at a time, trying to decide if he was still a functional human being.

It took him a moment to even remember what had happened. As he recalled the events of the previous night, he became overjoyed that he was still alive, despite the pain that gripped every muscle and joint of his body.

Quinlan pushed himself to a sitting position and leaned carefully against the rock tower, vowing never again to fall asleep on the Dunes of Mynar.

Once Quinlan had recovered himself, his sword, and his dagger, he made use of the rest of the day to travel, making sure to allow enough time to find refuge in one of the tower alcoves. Now, when the night calls of the penthomoths filled the air, he shivered.

The next morning he climbed higher up the tower and spotted a river that snaked its way through the towers from the east, its banks green with vegetation. He could also see the coast and Chesney Isle in the distance.

Delighted that his journey was nearing an end, he climbed down and hurried in the direction of the river, determined to make it out of the Dunes of Mynar by nightfall. The sun seemed to travel much faster that day, however, and he was forced to spend yet another night in this bizarre land.

That evening, the howling of a strong wind added to the usual Mynar night sounds. Just as Quinlan was dozing off into sleep, a thunderous *thump* shook the ground and the tower where he lay. Not long afterward, he heard a penthomoth's cry and shuddered. Then he heard another cry and another and another, all from the same direction. All through the night the creature trumpeted, keeping Quinlan from sleep.

By daybreak, the cries of the penthomoth were much less frequent, though they did not stop. This puzzled Quinlan, who had never heard that trumpet sound in the daylight. Climbing down from the tower, he set out toward the coast, eager to have his feet on solid ground once more. His northwesterly trek brought him closer to cries, which seemed to come from a point slightly ahead and to the right.

Just as he reached the place where the cry of the penthomoth was its loudest, the animal trumpeted once more, and the sound was almost like a plea. Quinlan stopped and looked toward his right, anxious to move on, but also compelled to find out what had happened. Perhaps he could safely get a better look at the terrifying monster that had nearly devoured him just three nights ago.

Quinlan veered off and carefully made his way toward the sounds of the monster. He quickly realized that he was traveling toward one of the fallen towers and that its toppling must have been what he heard during the night.

Quinlan studied the length of the prone tower ahead of him but saw nothing out of the ordinary. He ventured closer, carefully watching the sand for any movement. On its side, the width of the tower seemed much larger, still towering at least fifteen feet above him at places. The top half of the falling tower had splayed the sand out like a wave, forming a kind of valley around it. Large fragments of the stone spire had broken off and were strewn about the sand valley.

Quinlan made his way around the top end of the massive stone structure, where the soil, a couple of trees, and most of the vegetation had been uprooted and cast into the sand. Finally, on the other side of the tower, Quinlan spotted the source of the strange commotion. Down in the sand valley lay a large animal. One of its hind legs was pinned beneath a six-foot fragment of fallen stone.

The scattered sand gave evidence that the creature had tried for hours to dig its way out, but for some reason it had been unsuccessful. Now it lay on its side, exhausted and perfectly still except for deep, ragged breaths.

Realizing the penthomoth could not see him from its current position, Quinlan ventured a little closer, gawking at one of the strangest creatures he had ever seen—though it wasn't nearly the monster his imagination and the murky moonlight had made it out to be a few nights earlier.

The well-muscled body was the size of a large horse, with powerful legs angled so its body mass stayed low to the ground. The feet were wide and webbed, with large digging claws—clearly capable of moving buckets of sand in one swipe. The creature was hairless except for short, sand-colored fur covering its body and head.

The head, in fact, was what shocked Quinlan the most. What he had thought were tentacles were actually hairless trunks like that of an elephant, only more slender. Five of them waved from its face—one in the middle, bracketed by two short tusks, and two on either side. Quinlan looked into the open mouth for the rows of razor-sharp teeth he had imagined, but he saw only something resembling the teeth of a hound.

Having satisfied his curiosity about the animal, Quinlan turned to leave, but the penthomoth moaned a pathetic cry that tugged on his heart. He turned back, wishing now that he hadn't come. He slowly descended into the sand valley and walked around the pinned animal, giving it a wide berth. When he came within its field of view, the animal lurched and tried to scramble to its feet, then cried out in pain. Blood oozed from its leg and into the sand around it.

Still six paces away, Quinlan knelt to get a better look. The animal gradually calmed and settled its head back to the sandy bed, the trunks moving only slightly. Its gold-colored eyes followed Quinlan as he crept closer, staying just beyond the reach of the trunks.

Dare I go any closer? he wondered, remembering the strength of those quirky appendages. When he could not muster the nerve to go closer, the penthomoth moaned and reached out with its center trunk. Quinlan tentatively reached out and touched it. The penthomoth moaned again, and Quinlan's heart pounded. He fully expected the animal to grab him and eat him, but it didn't. It lay still and allowed him to come even closer.

Quinlan put his hand on the animal's flank and felt its chest rise and fall with each breath. Then it reached back with one trunk and gently touched his shoulder.

"You're not such a horrible monster after all, are you?" Quinlan said, and the animal gently cried out in agreement. He stroked it a couple of times, then went to where the stone fragment had pinned its legs to see if there was anything he could do to help. He felt beneath the animal's pinned leg and realized why it had been unable to free itself. About six feet below the surface of the surrounding sand was a solid rock floor. As the penthomoth had dug, the stone fragment had apparently settled deeper and deeper, pinning him firmly between the rock fragment and the stone floor.

Quinlan was at a loss as to what to do. The rock was simply too large to move, and the solid stone beneath made digging deeper impossible.

He went back to the head of the penthomoth. "You're in quite a fix, big fella." He stroked the animal again, and it just looked at him sadly out of the corner of its eyes. Quinlan opened his water bottle and poured a little water into the mouth of the exhausted animal. It lifted its head and lapped up the precious liquid, then moaned and settled back down.

Quinlan pondered what to do. He couldn't stay here, but leaving the animal to die of hunger or exposure was unthinkable.

"I'm sorry, big fella." Quinlan took out his dagger and set the blade against the penthomoth's throat. The animal seemed to know what was about to happen, but it stayed perfectly still. Quinlan had hunted animals of this size many times before, often ending their lives in just this way when an arrow had not fully done its job. He put a firm hand on the animal's cheek, took a deep breath, and readied himself...but for some reason he couldn't follow through.

Shaking his head, he returned the knife to its sheath. "Sorry, fella. I guess I'm not much help to you." The center trunk lifted up and rested across his chest as if to say, "It's all right."

Quinlan climbed out of the sand valley and retraced his steps. As he picked his way through the vegetation at the top of the fallen tower, an idea began forming in his mind.

He searched among the uprooted trees until he found one about fifteen feet long and as thick as his arm. Using his sword as an ax, he chopped off the flimsy upper portion, then cut away the branches until he had created a sturdy ten-foot pole. He carried it back to where the penthomoth lay and slid back down into the sand valley. After digging down far enough to stand on the stone floor, Quinlan wedged one end of the pole into a small space between the rock and the stone floor next to the penthomoth's leg. He pushed the pole through a short way and lifted the lever upward. It took all his might and multiple tries, but finally the large rock fragment lifted ever so slightly.

The penthomoth must have felt the ease in pressure, for it yanked its leg out, then screamed and glared at Quinlan. Quinlan quickly dropped the pole, realizing that being trapped in a sand pit with a hungry, injured wild beast was a precarious situation. He slowly backed away, but the penthomoth came after him, wrapping its trunks around him before he could draw his sword. Quinlan struggled, but the trunks were too strong as they pulled him toward its gaping mouth.

At the last moment, a long tongue came out and slurped across Quinlan's face. It felt disgusting, but it was far from deadly. Quinlan started to laugh as the penthomoth finally released him.

"Who's going to believe this story?" he said as he stroked the beast a few times.

The penthomoth made a sound similar to its scream, only softer. It turned and started licking its injured leg.

"Take care of yourself, big fella." Quinlan turned and climbed out of the sand valley. The penthomoth tried to climb out after him, but the injured leg hindered its efforts. Quinlan reached down a hand, and two of the trunks wrapped around his forearm. He dug in his heels, and though he slid and sank in the sand, the extra leverage was enough to help the animal out of the valley. It limped a few paces and lay down.

Quinlan dug his way back out of the sand and walked over to the penthomoth, which lay quietly as Quinlan gently lifted its leg. As far as he could tell, the bone was not broken, though the hide had been scraped and cut and the muscle seemed torn. The injury looked very painful.

Quinlan shook his head, upset with himself that he had ever come

to find out what the ruckus was all about. He needed to be on his way, but he also felt obligated to help this animal, which had attached itself to him in a strange way.

"Well," he finally said, "if I'm going to help you, you must have a name. What will it be?"

The penthomoth looked at him with expressive gold eyes, then took to licking its wound again.

"I think your name will be Kalil. It means 'friend.'" The penthomoth trumpeted approval, and Quinlan laughed.

Quinlan drank from his water bottle, then offered another drink to Kalil. He collected some leaves and berries from the shrubs that had fallen with the stone tower and offered them to Kalil, who devoured them immediately. Later Quinlan killed a couple of brown snakes, and Kalil ate them too.

"Is there anything you won't eat?" he asked his strange new friend. "Besides me, that is?" In response, Kalil stroked him with his trunks, something Quinlan was slowly getting used to. The animal actually seemed to be an affectionate and intelligent creature.

Quinlan stayed with Kalil the rest of the day except for when he made a trip to the river a short distance north of them to fill his water bottle. Kalil was sleeping when he returned, and Quinlan was reminded that the animal was not only exhausted but also nocturnal, accustomed to sleeping during the day. Quinlan considered moving on while it slept, but it was already too late to make the sea today, and he wasn't sure Kalil could survive on his own. So he spent the rest of the day hunting for food, then lay down beside Kalil to sleep.

The peace of the evening did not last long. Quinlan felt the sand beneath him shift and move, so he jumped up. He dove a few feet to another place in the sand, but that moved too. No matter where he went, the sand seemed to shift all around him. Then trunks just like Kalil's began to rise up out of the sand.

"Kalil!" he shouted to his penthomoth friend, but the animal seemed comatose.

Two penthomoths simultaneously rose up out of the sand, surrounding Quinlan. They growled and bared their teeth in a way he had never heard nor seen Kalil do. In this state, the animals were terrifying. Sinuous trunks moved slowly as if looking for the perfect place to grasp their victim. Muscles rippled in anticipation of the attack. The penthomoths crouched low, preparing to pounce.

Quinlan reached over and jostled Kalil just as one of the penthomoths lunged for him and grabbed his legs. Another grabbed his arms, and he thought he was about to be torn in half.

Just then an ear-piercing trumpet blasted, and the penthomoths hesitated. Kalil limped toward Quinlan, growling—but not at him. The penthomoth holding his arms released him just as Kalil wrapped his trunks around his torso. Kalil trumpeted again, and the other penthomoth released his legs. Kalil gently set Quinlan down and turned to face the other animals. After a volley of snarls and growls, they fled to seek easier prey.

When it was all over, Quinlan breathed a sigh of relief. "Thank you, friend," he said when Kalil returned and nuzzled him.

Quinlan continued to feed Kalil over the next few days until the animal was able to start using his leg again.

When Quinlan traveled toward the river and on to the sea, the penthomoth stayed with him.

Quinlan waited by the sea near the river's broad mouth for three days, keeping an eye on Chesney Isle a fair distance offshore. While he waited, Kalil grew stronger and was soon hunting and foraging on his own. Quinlan was now certain the animal would survive back in its habitat—a relief because he knew he couldn't take Kalil on the next leg of his journey.

On the morning of the fourth day, Quinlan finally spotted a small boat coming from the island. Quinlan saw violet light through the crystal coin and knew the boat was for him.

Two Silent Warriors pulled the boat within a few feet of the shore and motioned for Quinlan just as Kalil, who had been foraging in the brush along the river, came trumpeting from the trees.

"Hurry—get in!" One of the Silent Warriors drew his sword. "These creatures can't swim."

"It's all right. He's a friend." Quinlan walked toward the romping penthomoth, who bounded closer, then leaped into the air.

"Watch out!" the Silent Warrior yelled, but Kalil landed just in front of Quinlan and ducked low before him, crying in sad tones.

Quinlan stroked Kalil, and the animal wrapped his trunks around him. Quinlan pointed inland. "Kalil, you can't come with me. You must return to the dunes."

Kalil slowly released him, fell to the ground, and rolled over for Quinlan to stroke his chest. Quinlan obliged, then stood up. "I've got to go, Kalil. Go home!"

Quinlan started wading toward the boat. Kalil turned back on his feet and tried to follow. He trumpeted sadly and splashed in the water as Quinlan climbed into the boat. As the warriors began to row, Kalil actually plunged into the sea and began to paddle toward them.

"Remarkable," one of the warriors said.

When Kalil realized he could not catch them, he turned back to shore, shook himself, and trumpeted a woeful cry.

Quinlan felt a little woeful himself. He was surprised how quickly Kalil had become attached to him…and he to Kalil.

EIGHTEEN

A WARRIOR'S WORLD

 The Silent Warriors didn't row straight to Chesney Isle. They traveled around the northern tip of the island and into a small harbor. Quinlan was surprised to see a gallant three-masted ship waiting there, with sails ready to be set for sea. *So Chesney never was the destination,* he thought. Anticipation mixed with anxiety as he wondered where his journey would take him next.

Once aboard the ship, Quinlan briefed the captain on what he had learned from spying on the Shadow Warrior tent back in the Tara Hills. His information was received with the utmost attention, and he was asked to write out a full report of the conversation and his observations on parchment.

Four slightly seasick days later, Quinlan disembarked at a long dock leading to yet another island. His footsteps echoed on the planks as he followed his guides along the dock and down a path leading to the island's heart. There Quinlan discovered an entire garrison of Silent Warriors and a training camp the likes of which he had never seen. The camp took up nearly half of the large island. There were fighting arenas, obstacle courses, simulated shops and streets, cliffs, and some places he could not name. He was as deep into the secret world of warriors as he could possibly be.

Quinlan was amazed at how simply saying yes to the Prince one evening on Mount Resolute had dramatically changed his life. He thought of Burkfield, where Tav still lived in comfortable ignorance, and was thankful to be free from the mundane walk many Knights of the Prince chose.

Quinlan was brought before a large fellow who looked like he could wrestle a full-grown penthomoth and win. He suspected the warrior's bronzed skin revealed untold hours of outdoor training at this secret camp in uncharted Great Sea waters.

"I'm Rafe," the warrior said tersely. "Taras said you might be coming, although I expected you earlier."

"I had a bit of a delay in the Dunes of Mynar," Quinlan replied.

"Yes, we saw you enter, and usually a delay there means a person doesn't come out. You're fortunate." Rafe scrutinized Quinlan. "I will oversee your training. You should know that failure to master one aspect of training is failure to master all, and you cannot leave until you master all. The easy preliminary training Taras began I will perfect and complete. In the end, the warrior-spirit test will determine if you are worthy. If you can't accept this, you must leave immediately." Rafe squinted at Quinlan. "Choose now."

Quinlan did not hesitate. "I traveled from one end of the kingdom to the other to come to this point," he said. "I'll not walk away now."

"Perhaps." Rafe turned on his heel. "But you may wish you had. Follow me."

Rafe took Quinlan deeper into the camp, to a place where four warriors stood waiting.

"Gentlemen, this is Sir Quinlan, a recruit from Taras."

The veteran warriors all turned and eyed Quinlan. He felt small and insignificant in their presence and almost questioned his resolve, but the momentum of his earlier actions propelled him onward.

"This is Tarick. He'll be instructing you on weapons." The warrior nodded, and Quinlan responded likewise.

"Zeke is hand combat," Rafe continued. "Kird is reconnaissance and evasion. Moui is Shadow Warrior tactics, and I'll be instructing tactical and strategic maneuvers. Training begins at daybreak. You'll spend three hours with each instructor each day, with meals after every other session."

Rafe crossed his arms and glared at Quinlan. "Any questions?"

"No sir," Quinlan replied.

"Very well. We have time for one session today yet. Zeke, you take it."

"Yes sir." The warrior motioned for Quinlan to follow him.

That evening after Quinlan had eaten, he lay down exhausted, wondering how he would survive five training sessions each day. The hand combat session had reduced him to a sore bag of bones and bruised muscles.

Rafe was right. Quinlan's training with Taras had been simple and easy by comparison.

The days that followed seemed like weeks, and the weeks seemed like days. Quinlan knew he was improving, but he had no idea what standards Rafe was measuring him by.

Quinlan learned the art of the sword and became a master. Tarick also taught him daggers and knives, multiple polearms and axes, and a sundry of blunt weapons. From Zeke, he learned hand combat, both with and without daggers. He recognized that Lilam had used a style similar to one of the three Zeke was teaching him. Zeke's training was the most intense and exhausting, for it required great physical stamina and strength and therefore emphasized physical conditioning.

Reconnaissance and evasion, on the other hand, was more of a mental challenge, and Kird took this training to a whole new level, schooling him extensively in Shadow Warrior tactics and how to counter them. Quinlan discovered he had a mind and a body for this kind of work, and the sessions with Kird quickly became his favorites—along with Rafe's sessions in tactics and strategy. Though the physical training was a critical part of the process, Quinlan came to believe that the mental prowess of a warrior was his best weapon—and defense.

The training continued through the rest of the summer and into the fall, and it didn't stop for the mild island winter. After nine months in the warrior camp, Quinlan had learned much—though compared to his instructors, he felt he was still just beginning. One spring afternoon near the end of his training, Quinlan was heading for the meal tent when he spotted a familiar face.

"Taras! It is good to see you," Quinlan said with a broad smile. "It's been such a long time."

Taras smiled. "It is good to see you too, Sir Quinlan. Rafe tells me your training is going well."

"Really?" Quinlan asked, genuinely curious. "I really wouldn't know. I just try to do my best each day and hope that I'm improving."

Taras nodded. "It's our way." Quinlan laughed and nodded his agreement.

"It was my intention to be one of your instructors," Taras told him. "But after our discovery at the Tara Hills—and especially after the courier delivered your report to headquarters—I was called away on a mission. By the way, your discovery at the Shadow Warrior camp was... significant, to say the least."

"Thank you," Quinlan replied.

"But as of now, I will be overseeing the remainder of your training."

"I look forward to it," Quinlan said, not sure if life was going to get easier or harder.

"As a matter of fact, I have a training exercise for you right now." Taras motioned for Quinlan to follow.

"I...ah...the meal—" Quinlan stammered. His stomach was howling in hunger.

"The best training happens when you simulate real conditions." Taras spoke over his shoulder. "Do you think you'll always have a night's rest and food in your stomach before each mission?"

Definitely harder, Quinlan told himself as he hurried to catch up to Taras.

They walked to the outskirts of the training camp, where Taras pointed toward the uninhabited half of the island. Quinlan had never been there, but he knew it covered many miles.

"I have a warrior somewhere out there." Taras's voice had transformed from friend to detached instructor. "I want you to find him, do reconnaissance, and report back to me."

Quinlan stared at the tangle of foliage before him, then looked up at Taras. "There are only three hours of light left."

"It might take you three hours; it might take you a month. When you've found him and reconned, report back." Taras turned and walked away, but stopped. "By the way, he's one of our best, so be careful."

Quinlan steeled himself, then plunged into the underbrush. He wanted to cover as much ground as possible while the light was still available.

After about an hour of traveling, he realized that all his training was paying off. His movements were natural and his methods instinctual. With every foot of ground he covered, his eyes scanned effortlessly for signs of a prior passerby.

After the second hour, he climbed a hill and charted his progress, mapping out a mental grid of the remaining island based on how far he had already come. He shook his head over the task before him. It seemed nearly impossible, given the area he needed to cover.

Quinlan finally made the mental leap to the reality that he would need to search for days. His first priority was a source of water, then food. The island had enough edible vegetation to allow him to stay on mission without having to hunt. Surviving on grasses and berries wasn't a pleasant prospect, but the quicker he could find his target, the quicker he would be back to solid meals.

By late afternoon of the second day, Quinlan had an epiphany that made him feel like an ignoramus. He had been so immersed in training with the Silent Warriors over the past months that he had completely forgotten about the crystal coin.

I could have been out and back before sundown last night, he told himself.

He made his way to the nearest hill with a good vantage point, then looked through the forgotten crystal coin for the first time in months. He glassed the entire island, looking for that subtle glimmer of violet that would reveal his target to him. He saw nothing but rocks, vines, and fresh spring foliage—no glimmers at all.

When his eyes came to the northern coastline, however, he did spot a bright white light. This surprised him until he lowered the coin and realized he could see the same spot with his naked eye.

"A fire?" Quinlan pondered out loud. "That seems rather obvious. Maybe this warrior isn't nearly as good as Taras thinks he is."

Quinlan reset his camouflage and hurried in the direction of the fire. The closer he came to the coastline, however, the more slowly and silently he moved. As a precaution, he assumed that his target had set the fire to draw him in and was really waiting in ambush. Therefore, Quinlan carefully circled the fire, actually looking for his target at a peripheral distance of a hundred paces. He peered through the crystal coin again and again, trying to spot the warrior, but all he could see was the distant glow of the fire.

When his search came up empty, Quinlan felt he had no choice but to investigate the fire itself. He had decided that this warrior was either incredibly brilliant or incredibly careless. A visit to the campfire would reveal which was true.

Quinlan crawled the last one hundred paces on his belly more quietly than when he had entered the Shadow Warrior camp. At thirty paces away, he could make out a lone hooded figure sitting on a log near the fire. The smell of wood smoke hung in the air, along with another, more enticing aroma—roasted meat.

Quinlan tried the crystal coin again, but the kasilite crystal seemed to amplify the firelight, blinding him to anything else. Quinlan lowered the crystal coin and peered more closely at the figure by the fire.

Could be a decoy, he thought. He redirected his focus to his surroundings, suspecting the warrior was looking for him. He nearly retreated at that point but decided to go just a little closer. To be safe, he adjusted his direction so he could approach the figure directly from behind. When he was within fifteen paces, he peered closely at the lone figure to make sure it wasn't just a stuffed tunic and trousers.

"Why don't you come and warm yourself by the fire, Quinlan," the man said without turning around.

Quinlan lowered his head. *Impossible!* he thought. Then he realized this could be a trick. Maybe the warrior was calling out randomly, just to get him to reveal his location.

"Fifteen paces, directly behind me," the warrior said. "I've been waiting for you all day."

Quinlan shook his head in defeat, pushed to his feet, and walked the last few paces into the light of the fire. As he did, the meat smell hit him hard, and his empty stomach clenched.

"How did you know?" Quinlan sat down on a log opposite the warrior and began removing grass and branches from his clothing. He now saw that the man was roasting chunks of meat on a stick over the fire.

"That's not important." The warrior stood and walked over to Quinlan. "Here…eat."

Quinlan hesitated, still not quite sure how to respond. Slowly he reached to take the roasting stick.

"Thank you." He raised it to his lips and nibbled the hot, succulent meat.

"Well," he said when he had finished the first bite, "since I've miserably failed this training exercise, what happens now? A repeat?"

The warrior reached down and put another log on the fire, then returned to his previous seat. By now the sun was down, and night was upon them. Quinlan looked across the dancing flames into the darkened face of the hooded warrior. He did not recognize him as anyone he had seen at camp, and yet…

"You haven't failed," the warrior said. "Not yet."

Now Quinlan was really confused. After nine months of intensive training in the world of Silent Warriors, he thought he had grown used to their mysterious ways, but apparently not. It was as if there was always something more to know, learn, try, and discover. Everything always seemed just out of his reach. He could never quite feel comfortable.

Quinlan finished chewing another delicious bite and looked across the fire once more at his companion. He couldn't help feeling that he had met this warrior before.

"Do I know you, sir?" Quinlan finally asked.

The man threw back his hood. His eyes reflected the bright flames of the fire.

"Now that is an important question," he said, "one that all Arrethtraens should ask. *Do* you know me, Quinlan?"

Quinlan sat motionless, mesmerized by the gaze of the man. Suddenly chills flowed up and down his spine, and he began to tremble. He hardly dared consider what his heart already knew. *Could it be?* he wondered. *Could it truly be?*

"My Prince," he whispered.

The Prince stood once more and walked around to him. Quinlan dropped the roasted meat into the fire and fell to one knee. He dared not look into the face of his Prince, and yet he dared not look away. He was speechless before the One he had vowed to serve.

"Yes," the majestic voice said. "It is I. Rise up."

Quinlan slowly stood. His eyes welled up for a hundred reasons, yet he could only think of one. Before him was the One who had died for all of Arrethtrae, who had come back to save as many as would follow Him, who would one day take His rightful place as ruler of all the kingdom. He had chosen to meet this night with Quinlan, a young man with a failed past...a man who lacked so much.

"Do you know who you are, Quinlan?" the Prince asked gently.

Quinlan hesitated, vaguely remembering the words of Taras from many months before. *Lesson one—know who you are...*

He straightened. "I am and always shall be Your servant, my Lord."

"Yes...and so much more. You are my friend and my brother, fellow heir to the kingdom as a son of the King. Do you believe this?" the Prince asked.

Quinlan faltered, for what he felt was something so completely different. For the first time in many months, Quinlan felt his cheek tense up. He struggled for words.

"I believe it because you speak it, my Prince, and therefore I know it to be true regardless of what I feel, for You speak only truth."

The Prince put his hands on each side of Quinlan's neck. "Yes, now live what you believe. You need not be afraid...of anything!"

The warmth of the Prince's hands radiated throughout Quinlan's neck and face, and he felt the tense muscles ease. The Prince smiled. Quinlan let go of all that he was and became all that he wanted to be…simply because the King made it so.

The Prince lowered his hands. "Do you know why you are here, on the island of Silent Warriors?"

"To train so I can serve You as one of the knights of the Swords of Valor," Quinlan replied.

Lesson two—know who you want to become.

"Look into the fire," the Prince commanded, and Quinlan obeyed.

"Now close your eyes. What do you see?"

"Nothing, my Lord," Quinlan said. "How can I see anything with my eyes closed?"

"Keep looking," the Prince said patiently.

Then Quinlan saw it. He had never thought of "seeing" with his eyes closed, but now he saw a remnant image of the glowing fire. The more he concentrated, the clearer it became; then it slowly faded away.

He opened his eyes and looked up at the Prince. "I saw the glow of the fire."

"Much like the glow you see when you look at warriors through the kasilite medallion." The Prince turned and walked a few paces away.

Quinlan thought about what he'd said and realized it was true.

"Your eyes can see them the same way," the Prince said with His back to Quinlan.

Quinlan was stunned as he considered the ramifications of possessing such a skill.

"Only the commander of the Swords of Valor sees like this." The Prince turned and pointed at him. "You, Quinlan."

Quinlan's eyes widened. What was He saying? Surely not… Everything in him wanted to deny what the Prince was asking of him, but he dared not.

The Prince walked toward him once more. "I have called you and equipped you. Through me you are more than a conqueror."

Quinlan bowed his head. "My Lord, what you are asking of me

seems impossible. I had hoped to once more serve with the unit, but the others will never accept me as their leader. Not after what I've done."

Quinlan looked up into the Prince's compelling eyes. He found no release from the call.

"Will you go and live what you believe?" the Prince asked.

Quinlan took a deep breath, then submitted to the call that demanded the impossible. He bowed his head. "I will go, my Prince." Speaking the words made everything real, and he established his heart to be confident in Him.

"Then it is done, and you are ready to return to Arrethtrae." The Prince placed a firm hand on Quinlan's shoulder. "Be strong, for I am strong in you."

The Prince turned and began to walk away. Quinlan just stood and watched him, realizing that in those few moments he had changed forever. Ten years of special training could not have done what the Prince had just accomplished for Quinlan. He would never be the same nor live in past failures ever again.

"My Lord," he called after the Prince's retreating figure, "what of the warrior-spirit test Rafe spoke of?"

The Prince stopped and looked back.

"It is already done. You were worthy when you fed and cared for me. That is why I allowed you to come here, and that is why you will be commander of the Swords of Valor."

"When did *I* feed you and care for you, my Lord?" Quinlan asked, befuddled.

The Prince just smiled, placed the hood back onto his head, and walked into the night. The smoke of the fire wafted up into Quinlan's eyes, and he shut them for a moment. As he did, he saw the glowing outline of the Prince behind his eyelids and marveled. But the light was not violet. It was bright white. Would it always be thus? he wondered. How could he discern between Silent Warrior and Shadow Warrior if the glow was always white?

Quinlan opened his eyes and reached for the crystal coin in his pocket. He lifted it to his eyes and nearly dropped the coin. He had to squint in order to see, because the light emanating from the Prince was brighter than the sun.

Quinlan lowered the coin, and the blackness of night swallowed the regal form of the Prince once again. ▣

NINETEEN

RETURN TO ARRETHTRAE

 Quinlan and Taras stood on the dock, gazing westward over the glittering expanse of the Great Sea. Somewhere on the other side was a kingdom and a King waiting for Quinlan—one day. The ship next to them was in its final stages of preparation for a voyage to Chesney Isle.

"If you'll wait," said Taras, "we have a ship that arrives and departs in three weeks. That one can take you closer to Mankin, where I've arranged for Kobalt to be waiting for you. I'm sorry the options aren't better, but there are certain missions we cannot change."

Quinlan shook his head with a smile and offered his arm in a farewell gesture. Burkfield weighed heavily on his mind, and waiting was not an option.

Taras grabbed his forearm and stared into Quinlan's eyes. "I understand," the Silent Warrior said. "The Prince has that effect on people. You've done well, knight."

"Thank you, Taras. I assume I'll be hearing from you?"

Taras nodded. "Gather the team, but be careful. We're watching Lucius watch them. The Shadow Warriors know the danger."

"And if the knights won't follow?" Quinlan swung his small pack onto his shoulder.

"Every man chooses his own path." Taras turned back up the dock. "If they don't follow, you'll know what to do."

Four days later, Quinlan found himself on the sandy shores of Arrethtrae near the Dunes of Mynar. He was a different man, but no one else knew it yet. The Prince had equipped him with skills to match his passion for service—service that would begin today. Quinlan needed the best knights for his mission, so he would seek for those he knew to be the best—no matter what they thought of him.

"But I think I shall start and end with a friend," he mused as he looked southward toward Norwex.

He walked a few paces down the beach, remembering his time in the Dunes of Mynar with Kalil. He smiled a little sadly, wondering if the beast had successfully assimilated back into the wild.

He didn't have to wait long to find out.

The next instant, a familiar multitoned trumpet sounded. The bushes shook and split as a fearsome creature burst through and charged toward Quinlan.

Quinlan froze, unsure what to do. He drew his sword and held it firmly at his side—just in case. Seconds later, the penthomoth plowed into Quinlan, wrapped its five trunks about him and licked him until Quinlan's neck and shoulders were wet with saliva.

"All right, Kalil," Quinlan laughed. "It's good to see you too. I can't believe you waited for me."

Kalil mumbled joyfully and rolled on his back for Quinlan to scratch his belly.

The journey back through the Dunes of Mynar was uneventful, though Quinlan appreciated Kalil's protective presence during the sandy trek. The animal even seemed to have overcome its nocturnal instincts so it could live in the same space of the day as Quinlan. But what would happen once they reached the borders of Mynar?

After four days of steady travel, they reached the hills that separated Mynar from the region south of it. Quinlan looked over at Kalil, wondering what to do. Kalil looked back with loyal golden eyes that seemed to say, what are we waiting for?

Quinlan shrugged and started up the first hill. Kalil stayed right beside him. When they reached the plains beyond, Quinlan realized he would have no small difficulty traveling through Arrethtrae and conducting secret missions with a penthomoth at his side.

"Well, Kalil," he said, "if you're going to stay with me, you're going to need some serious training."

As they traveled south, Quinlan worked to train Kalil and was amazed at the animal's ability to understand and respond. He used voice commands to teach him all of the tricks one might teach a hound. Through whistles and hand motions, he taught him to come or to disappear.

Disappearing, which meant leaving Quinlan, proved to be the most difficult trick for Kalil to master. Quinlan gradually lengthened the time he could spend away until he could go an entire day without seeing Kalil at all. It helped that the animal seemed to prefer the trees and brush to the open plains, apparently feeling more secure in closed-in areas that reminded him of his sandy den in the desert. That preference made traveling a little easier for Quinlan, who could travel in the open while Kalil was foraging and traveling under cover of vegetation.

One evening when they were nearly to Norwex, Quinlan lay down next to Kalil, musing at the difference between the two strange animals that had attached themselves to him. The more time he had spent with Bli, the more the paytha had become *his* master. But the more time he spent with Kalil, the more Quinlan became Kalil's master. Bli was as appealing as an animal could be, while Kalil was quite ugly, at least according to the kingdom's standards. But Bli had abandoned Quinlan when he chose the Prince, while Kalil followed him faithfully. Perhaps the difference was simply due to coincidence or the personalities of the creatures, but Quinlan couldn't help but wonder if there was something more involved.

The next morning, before the sun began spilling its vibrant rays over the distant horizon, Quinlan arrived at a familiar ranch home. As he knocked, he heard the clatter of pans and dishes as the morning meal was being prepared. The door opened, and there stood Lilam. One hand rested on the hilt of her sword, and the other was on her hip.

"You came back," she said a little doubtfully.

Quinlan nodded. "I said I would." He smiled. "Where I'm going, I'll need the best fighters in all of Arrethtrae, and I heard there was one here."

Lilam's lips slowly curled into a smile. She pushed the door open wider and called over her shoulder, "Set another place at the table, Aven." She looked back at Quinlan. "I'm glad to see you. Come in."

Quinlan's reunion with Lilam's family was joyful. And this time, though her parents were still hesitant, they admitted they could not keep Lilam from what seemed to be her destiny. While Quinlan was gone, apparently, Lilam had intensified her training with Master Kwi, and the skills she showed him were impressive. Her intelligence and assertive personality seemed a perfect fit for the Swords of Valor. Quinlan had no concerns about her being able to hold her own against the likes of Purcell—if he agreed to join the unit again.

By midafternoon, Quinlan and Lilam had said their farewells to her family and set their course toward the village of Mankin. When evening came they built a fire, and Quinlan asked Lilam to stand up and face him. "There's something I need to tell you," he said. "I thought about keeping it a secret, but I just don't think that would work."

Lilam raised an eyebrow. "What is it?"

"Someone else is going to be traveling with us."

"Well, I rather expected that," she said with a smirk.

"Believe me, this isn't like anything you would expect."

"Try me."

"Very well. Keep your eyes on me."

Quinlan whistled, and the bushes behind Lilam parted. Quinlan held out his hand to signal a quiet approach and Kalil sank low to the ground, creeping up behind Lilam. Quinlan even had second thoughts as he watched the powerful muscles tense as for an attack.

"Now I need you to turn around—slowly." Quinlan stood ready to calm both Lilam and Kalil if need be.

Lilam slowly turned around until she stood face to trunks with Kalil. To Quinlan's surprise, she did not jump, or scream, or even gesture. Instead, she reached out a hand. Kalil reached out with his central trunk and sniffed, then wrapped the trunk around her wrist.

"He's amazing," Lilam murmured without taking her eyes of off the penthomoth. "What's his name?"

"Kalil. It means 'friend.'" Quinlan went to stand beside Kalil and rested a hand on the animal's back. "This is your monster penthomoth from the Dunes of Mynar."

Lilam reached over to rub Kalil's sand-colored head, and the penthomoth groaned with pleasure. Quinlan smiled, glad his friends had become friends too.

Nine days later, Quinlan and Lilam arrived on the outskirts of Mankin, a small city tucked away between the Tara Hills and the Great Sea. After ordering Kalil to stay in the woods outside town, they hiked into Mankin. They asked about stables, but only the town prefect had them, and Quinlan was quite sure Kobalt would not be there.

"The blacksmith sometimes keeps horses," the owner of the weaver shop offered.

They made their way toward the blacksmith's shop, expecting the familiar smell of red-hot iron, the sound of pounding hammers, and the sight of white steam. When they arrived, however, the coals of the forge were cold and the tools were all put away.

"Quite odd how the shop is open and unattended," Quinlan said.

He nodded to Lilam that they should leave, but then they heard the clop of hoofs coming their way. A large man appeared from around the right corner of the shop with three horses in tow.

"Kobalt!" Quinlan hurried over to his steed, who nickered in recognition. The animal looked well fed and groomed.

"He is a battle horse now," the man said in an accent Quinlan had never heard before. He handed the reins to Quinlan.

"Thank you, sir," Quinlan said. He closed his eyes for an instant and saw a violet afterimage.

The warrior handed another set of reins to Lilam. "For you, Lady Lilam. Her name is Adira. It means 'strong.'"

Lilam took the reins with a look of disbelief. "How did you—"

"You will need her in the days to come," the warrior said.

"Thank you, sir," she finally managed to say.

The man went to shut the doors of the shop.

"Are you closing so early?" Quinlan asked.

The warrior turned. "I have been here many years, and now my work is done." He looked to the horizon, then crossed over to his own steed. "The days are short, and I must go to prepare for them."

He gave them a salute as he mounted. "The King reigns!"

"And His Son!" Quinlan and Lilam answered as he rode away.

"Well, Lilam," Quinlan said as he mounted Kobalt for the first time in many months. "Now the search begins."

Lilam swung a leg over Adira. "Lead on, Commander."

Quinlan looked at her, a little taken aback, but she just waited.

"To Blackbridge…and the scoundrel who waits there," he said with a smile. He slapped Kobalt's reins and they launched their steeds south.

Commander, Quinlan said to himself as he rode. *That's going to take some getting used to.* 🔲

TWENTY

GATHERING OF SWORDS

 Quinlan and Lilam arrived in Blackbridge on a warm spring afternoon and wondered how they would ever find the man they sought. The town was once his home, according to Taras, but he was used to living a secret life, and Quinlan was certain the secrecy would continue.

They approached the village square, where a crowd of people had gathered.

"Sticking an apple with a knife at thirty paces is impossible," a voice called out. "No one here believes you."

Quinlan dismounted and handed his reins to Lilam. "I'll be back in a minute." He stepped up behind the crowd and peered over heads and shoulders. In the midst of them, sitting on a stump and peeling an apple, was the very person he wanted to find.

Quinlan laughed to himself. *Secret life—sure.*

"You'll have to prove it," another person yelled.

"Why should I prove it to you?" Purcell calmly took a bite of the apple, and juice dripped down his scraggily beard. "I know I can do it."

"Aw, he's just blowin' smoke," the first man said. "Why don't you put your money where your mouth is?"

Purcell smiled. "I'm not a gambling man."

The man sneered. "See—just blowin' smoke!"

"But," Purcell continued, "since I know I can do it, it wouldn't be gambling, now would it?"

The man stepped forward and placed coins on the stump next to Purcell. "Two florins says you won't even come close." He turned to the crowd and grinned. Shouts of affirmation rose up.

Purcell grabbed a fresh apple and got to his feet. "Hold out your hand," he said.

Looking to the people for encouragement, the man slowly lifted his hand. Purcell put the apple in it.

"You hold the apple," he said. "If I hit it, you pay me four florins. If I miss, I pay you six."

The crowd muttered, and the man grew nervous. "I'm not risking my life for six florins." He slapped the apple back into Purcell's hand and grabbed his coins.

Purcell smiled and shrugged. He threw the apple into the air and caught it.

"Is there no one brave enough to take my challenge?" he yelled as he held up the apple.

There was no response except low murmurs from the crowd.

"Then I shall keep my knives in hand, and you will never—"

"I'll do it!" Quinlan shouted. Heads turned to see who had spoken.

Purcell jerked his own head around and squinted to see who had accepted his challenge. Quinlan stepped forward, and the crowd parted to let him through. He was surprised that Purcell didn't seem to recognize him. Evidently his full beard and strengthened body had changed his appearance significantly.

"Now here's a man of heart!" Purcell called out to the crowd, gesturing toward Quinlan.

"Not all would think so," Quinlan said.

At hearing Quinlan's voice, Purcell squinted again and peered closer. Recognition came slowly, but it came. Purcell's nostrils flared as anger filled his eyes.

Quinlan did not flinch. He reached out and took the apple from

Purcell and set it on his own left shoulder, just above his heart. The crowd began to buzz with excitement.

Purcell continued to stare intently at Quinlan for a moment, then turned and walked thirty paces. When he turned around, the crowd cleared a wide berth behind Quinlan.

Purcell lifted his knife and prepared to throw it. He made a quick motion as though he were making an attempt, then pulled up short of releasing the knife. Quinlan stood as steady as an oak tree. The onlookers held their breath in anticipation.

Purcell readied himself once more, then recoiled and released the razor-sharp knife on a trajectory that would carry it straight to the apple…or Quinlan's heart.

The crowd gasped as the knife flew, then hit—sending the apple careening over Quinlan's shoulder and onto the ground. The people erupted in thunderous applause. Quinlan bent to recover the apple and the knife, and walked over to Purcell. The two men glared at each other in silence for a moment.

"The Prince is calling, and the Swords of Valor are gathering," Quinlan said in a quiet, steady voice. "Those brave enough to fight again are meeting at Stockford in a fortnight."

Purcell glared. "Fighting beside an inexperienced squire who hardly knows which end of a sword is which isn't brave. It's suicide!"

Quinlan met Purcell's eyes a moment longer, then pulled the knife from the apple, flipped it into the air, and grasped the blade. He handed it to Purcell as he leaned close to him and spoke softly.

"When's the last time you saw a Shadow Warrior?"

Purcell's hard stare eased as he considered Quinlan's question. His silent response gave Quinlan the answer.

"That's what I thought. You don't think they've gone away, now, do you?" Quinlan turned up one corner of his mouth, realizing all evidence of his facial twitch was gone. "You're either losing your edge, or you're so far off the front line that you don't matter to them anymore."

He took a bite of the apple, turned to walk away, but hesitated and turned back. "Just in case you're interested, the man standing beside the blacksmith's shop"—he gestured with his head—"is not of this king-dom, and he's been watching you since I arrived."

Quinlan turned and walked to where Lilam stood holding the horses. As he was mounting up, Purcell called after him. "My knife could have just as easily pierced your heart. You took a big risk."

Quinlan settled into his saddle. He wheeled Kobalt around to face Purcell. "You threw the knife, Sir Purcell. What was the risk?" He slapped the reins and they bolted away, leaving puffs of dust where hoofs once were.

Quinlan now set their course for Castleridge. Each evening after the day's travel, he called for Kalil, and the penthomoth bounded joyfully into their camp. Now that they were riding horseback, Quinlan was sur-prised Kalil could keep up, but he seemed to have no trouble. The ani-mal seemed to know he was a stranger in a strange land and kept well hidden throughout the day, but he always appeared delighted to join them at night. Quinlan was amazed at the joy and comfort the animal's presence brought him.

After three days of travel, Quinlan and Lilam arrived in Castleridge, Sir Drake's city of origin. They found no trace of him there, but they did discover a lead that sent them to the neighboring town of Rossborough.

The haven at Rossborough had grown quickly and become a launch site for many missions for the Prince. Quinlan knew the knights here required the finest training—a job well suited to someone experienced and proficient with the sword.

"We're looking for a knight named Sir Drake," Quinlan asked of the haven leader when they arrived in Rossborough. "Do you know of him?"

The balding man smiled as he looked up from a parchment. "Of course. You'll find 'im near the stables with the wee ones."

"Wee ones?" Quinlan asked.

"Aye, the wee ones," the man said. "Tenderhearted bloke—not much for the sword, so we've got 'im teaching the wee ones."

"Must be a different Drake." Quinlan turned to leave.

"Large fellow?" the man asked. "Blond hair?"

Quinlan turned back. "Yes…"

"Wouldn't dare take him into battle, but he sure does wonders with the little ones." He pointed. "You'll find him over there."

Quinlan furrowed his brow. "Thank you."

Following the man's directions, Quinlan and Lilam walked past a training arena crowded with knights engaged in a sparring contest. Shouts and cheers rose up with each cut and thrust. Quinlan stopped for a moment to admire the intensity of the fighting. Then he looked about, spotted the stables, and walked that way. Near a fence, he saw a large fellow kneeling in front of a dozen or so young children. Each child clutched a wooden sword and wore a tunic that bore the mark of the Prince. Even from a distance, Quinlan had no doubt their teacher was indeed the mighty Sir Drake.

Quinlan and Lilam approached from behind him and watched the children's faces as they became enamored with a story Drake was telling them. Punctuating his tale with broad gestures, the big man told them about the Prince's encounter with the Dark Knight before he revealed himself as the Son of the King. At one point, Drake drew his sword and began to reenact the epic duel that had determined the fate of the kingdom.

"The battle between the evil Dark Knight and the good Prince raged on." Drake swished at the air with his sword. "The rain poured down, and the Dark Knight advanced. The Prince stumbled over a rock and fell to the ground!" Drake keeled over dramatically, and the children gasped.

At that moment, Quinlan jumped into the scene, his black kerchief pulled over the lower part of his face. He held his sword toward Drake's chest and exclaimed in an evil voice, "Now I will kill you and rule all of Arrethtrae."

Drake looked up, stunned by the sudden appearance of a dramatic partner, but Quinlan wasted no time in keeping the drama going. He executed a vertical cut straight toward Drake's head, and the children yelled for their teacher to move.

At the last second, and much to Quinlan's relief, Drake executed a quick parry that deflected Quinlan's blade. The sword tore into the ground to the left of Drake's shoulder. Drake rolled to his right and onto his knees, exposing his back to Quinlan.

Quinlan brought down another vertical cut, but Drake locked his sword above his head and caught Quinlan's blade with his own. He simultaneously rotated on one knee and exploded a horizontal slice that arced full circle around to Quinlan. Quinlan jumped back as the tip of Drake's sword flew past his chest. This gave Drake enough time to recover and reestablish his position.

"My Father loved you, and you spurned His love," Drake said with a voice that boomed across the camp.

The two men engaged again, and Quinlan could see the thrill of the fight in Drake's eyes. With each cut, slice, and parry, the intensity of the swordplay increased. Soon the knights from the training arena began to filter over and watch. Before long, every knight in the haven stood open-mouthed as the meek Sir Drake and this stranger demonstrated a level of swordsmanship they had never seen before.

Drake advanced with a sequence of powerful cuts that forced Quinlan into retreat. Then Drake executed a powerful slice, and Quinlan played the finale well. He stumbled backward onto the ground as his sword flew from his grip. Drake stood over him with his sword pointed at Quinlan's chest.

"My Father has postponed your judgment for now," he proclaimed. "Though your final destruction is yet before you, it *is* a certainty!"

The final moment hung in the air as if curtains were being dropped. The children applauded and shouted their glee, but the knights stood in awed silence. Drake sheathed his sword and reached a hand down to his unknown costar. Quinlan grabbed hold, and Drake lifted him to his feet.

"Whoever you are," Drake said soberly, "you've ruined me."

Quinlan removed the kerchief from his face. "I think you've been acting for more than just the children."

Drake turned and looked deeply into Quinlan's eyes. Recognition dawned, but he said nothing. Instead, he turned and beckoned for the children to gather around him. They came with wooden swords in hand, ready for action.

"Remember, children," he said, "it is the Prince and the Code that gives your sword its power. Never forget that. Learn the Code, and live it well."

The children's eyes were large and full of wonder that Quinlan knew would not soon diminish. Drake dismissed the children. Head lowered, he walked through the crowd of knights. They respectfully stepped aside. Quinlan followed him.

"I never imagined you as a teacher of children."

Drake didn't miss a beat. "Of such is the kingdom of the Prince."

They walked over to the fence, and Drake rested his elbows on top of it. Quinlan propped his right foot on one of the lower rails and took a breath, unsure how to start.

"You've improved." Drake turned to look at Quinlan. "Significantly."

Quinlan leaned against the fence. "I've relived that dreadful day a thousand times in my mind, wishing I could change the outcome. I don't know why things happened the way they did, but I do know the Prince still needs the Swords of Valor to ride for Him." Quinlan let his words take effect. "Lucius is advancing, and our brothers and sisters need our help. I've been made aware of a new scheme to destroy much of the work of the Knights of the Prince, and I can't just stand by and watch it happen."

Drake eased himself away from the fence and shook his head. "I'm done, Quinlan. With Sir Baylor gone, his work just can't go on."

Quinlan's heart sank. "If that is true, then the Dark Knight has indeed won."

Drake leaned on the fence again and looked away.

"Those who are willing are meeting at Stockford in ten days." Quinlan started to leave, then stopped. "Drake, this isn't my work or your work, or even Sir Baylor's work. It's the King's."

Drake turned and leaned his back against the fence, then crossed his arms in what seemed an unmovable posture.

Quinlan saluted, then moved on. He and Lilam recovered their steeds and headed for Greyloch and his last chance at recruitment. Thus far he didn't feel very successful.

♛ ♛ ♛

It took Quinlan and Lilam four days to travel to the seafaring village of Greyloch, on the coast just north of Cytra. Quinlan had learned from Drake that Kessler worked as a hand loading and unloading wares from the boats that frequented the harbor, so he figured the man wouldn't be too difficult to find.

The strong smell of fish hovered around them as they walked along the shore, avoiding the droppings of sea gulls that wheeled overhead. When they came upon a shirtless, well-muscled dock hand who whistled while carrying a burden that would have been a challenge for two men, they stopped. Quinlan motioned for Lilam to hold back.

Kessler dropped his load onto the deck of the boat and turned around just as Quinlan arrived at the dock. Without a hint of surprise, he stepped back up onto the dock and walked toward Quinlan. Quinlan wondered if perhaps he still hadn't recognized him.

"What took you so long?" Kessler wiped beads of sweat from his swarthy brow.

Now it was Quinlan's turn to look confused. He cocked his head to one side. Kessler walked right past Quinlan and on toward the shore.

"Coming?" Kessler said over his shoulder. He grabbed his shirt from the dock post and walked to where Lilam was standing. "I'm Kessler, miss. Pleased to meet you."

Lilam raised an eyebrow and stuck out her hand. "Lilam."

He nodded for her to walk with him. "He treating you well?" Kessler asked as she fell in step with him and continued down the walkway.

Lilam looked over her shoulder at Quinlan, who still stood with a perplexed look on his face.

She grinned at Kessler. "Mostly."

Quinlan ran and caught up with them. "Kessler, what's going on?"

Kessler laughed. "I'm the one who's supposed to ask that question."

"You—you seemed to know that I was coming. How?"

Kessler turned about to face Quinlan. He wiped his forehead again with a corner of his shirt, then put the garment on, his face uncharacteristically serious.

"Do you remember the first time I met you?"

"Yes," Quinlan replied. "You and the other knights fought off

Shadow Warriors on Mount Resolute. I just happened to have stumbled into the skirmish, as I remember."

Kessler shook his head. "That wasn't an accident. You were their target. I analyzed their attack—they came specifically for you. At first it made no sense to me at all, considering…well, considering your abilities."

Quinlan smiled, trying not to take too much offense at the comment.

Kessler continued. "But later, when Baylor said you were the fifth member of the Swords of Valor, I knew something was strange. Baylor hadn't picked you—I could see it in his eyes. Someone else had."

Kessler grinned. "So it wasn't a matter of if you would come, just a matter of when."

Kessler motioned for Quinlan and Lilam to follow as he led them toward a barrel-chested man who was yelling at two other hands to quicken their pace.

"Guthrie," Kessler shouted. "I'm off."

"What?" the man shouted. "You can't leave, Kessler. You're my best man. Take an hour and then finish up the day."

"Sorry, Guth," Kessler said. "I'm done for good. I told you the day would come. You can keep the day's wage."

Guthrie looked like he wanted to protest, but he just shook his head. As they walked by him, the man nodded.

"You take care of yourself, Kessler."

"And you, Cap."

They walked a few paces as Quinlan considered Kessler's words.

"We aren't meeting for another week," Quinlan said.

"I don't need a week. I'll come with you now," Kessler said. "After I clean up, of course," he said with a smile and winked at Lilam. "Are Purcell and Drake coming?"

"Doubtful."

Kessler put his hand on Quinlan's shoulder. "You might be surprised."

TWENTY-ONE

COMMON ENEMY, COMMON FRIEND

 Quinlan had chosen Stockford as a meeting place for one reason—its proximity to Burkfield. When Quinlan, Lilam, and Kessler arrived there two days ahead of time, Drake was waiting for them.

"What changed your mind?" Quinlan asked.

"I don't know," the large man said with a frown. "I tried to stay away, but I just couldn't. I guess it's the little ones—that's who I'm fighting for."

Quinlan slowly nodded. "Can't think of a better reason. Drake… Lilam. Lilam…Drake."

Drake tilted his head, and Lilam nodded.

They waited the next two days for Purcell. Each evening, Quinlan made a point of riding out to where Kalil waited. For now, he had decided to keep the penthomoth a secret from Kessler and Drake and anyone else they might meet. Kalil had learned to be as silent and stealthy as a Silent Warrior and had little difficulty staying out of sight. He didn't seem to mind waiting for Quinlan to appear, but his joy over their time together, even if it was just a few minutes, reminded Quinlan how good it was to have a friend.

When Purcell failed to show on the appointed day, the unit rode on to Burkfield without him. Everyone in the unit felt the oppression hidden behind the peaceful, prosperous facade.

"What's that?" Lilam pointed to a creature perched on a man's shoulder.

"It's a paytha," Quinlan replied. "They're nasty little things."

"They don't look it," Kessler said, watching the animal nuzzle next to its owner's neck.

The farther they rode into Burkfield, the more paythas they saw. In fact, the animals were everywhere, and not all of them rode on people's shoulders. Some leered from the corners of shops and skulked in alleyways. Quinlan gave them all wide berth.

The group made their way to the haven, but it looked practically abandoned. The other knights scouted about the haven grounds while Quinlan knocked and knocked on Sir Edmund's door. There was no answer.

"Sir Edmund?" Quinlan slowly opened the door and saw a man sitting at a table, his head between his hands.

"Sir Edmund," Quinlan repeated, wondering what was wrong.

The man slowly lifted his head and stared at Quinlan. "Can I help you?" he said somberly.

"Sir Edmund, it is I—Quinlan."

Edmund tilted his head, looking confused.

"Twitch," Quinlan said.

Slowly a weak smile lit across Sir Edmund's face. "Twitch…it's been a long time. You look—"

"Where are the other knights, sir?" Quinlan interrupted. "What's happened here?"

The smile on Edmund's face disappeared, and he seemed to awaken from his lethargic state.

"I tried, Twitch. I really, really tried." Edmund shook his head. "I even brought Sir Worthington in, but one by one I lost them all. I don't think there are any Knights of the Prince left in Burkfield. If there are, they don't care. I've failed, and now I must leave too."

Quinlan strode over to Edmund's table. "You can't leave yet, sir. I'm here to help you."

Edmund shook his head. "What could you possibly do, Twitch? I've spent the last two years fighting this decay, and now it's over. I'm leaving tomorrow. Perhaps some other haven leader will allow me to assist him."

Quinlan grabbed a chair sitting next to a wall and set it across the table from Edmund. He sat down so he could look directly into Edmund's eyes.

"Give me one month, Sir Edmund," he pleaded. "Promise me you'll stay for just one more month."

"Why? What difference would it make?" But Quinlan saw a glimmer of hope in the man's eyes.

"This is much bigger than you realize," Quinlan said. "Give me a chance, sir, and it may make all the difference in the kingdom."

Edmund stared at Quinlan for a moment. "What happened to you, Twitch? You're...different."

"I met the Prince, Sir Edmund, and He changes everything!"

A corner of Sir Edmund's mouth lifted, although Quinlan couldn't tell if the man really believed him.

"All right," Edmund said. "I'll wait one month. But I can't imagine what difference it's going to make."

"Thank you!" Quinlan reached across the table and grabbed Edmund's arm. Then he stood and walked toward the door.

"Quinlan," Edmund called after him.

Quinlan turned.

"I met Him once too," Edmund said with a distant smile.

"I know," Quinlan said. "I can tell. I always could tell."

They camped that evening near the banks of Jewel Lake. After his comrades had settled for the evening, Quinlan went to spend time with Kalil. The penthomoth met him with the usual enthusiasm, and Quinlan put him through some of the commands they had been practicing. Then, in the middle of an exercise, Kalil stiffened and stared into the underbrush.

At first, Quinlan assumed the animal had spotted a night creature.

But when Kalil remained motionless, Quinlan began to wonder. He lifted the crystal coin to his eyes and scanned the area. In the distance, a very faint violet glow was coming toward them.

Quinlan commanded Kalil to disappear and ducked into the bushes himself. When the Silent Warrior passed by, he followed him to the edge of their camp and watched as the warrior knelt and waited. Quinlan silently made his way up behind the warrior. When he was within ten paces, the Silent Warrior stood up.

"I see my training has paid off," the warrior said. "Not even Baylor could get that close."

Quinlan stepped out of the brush. "It's good to see you, Taras."

Taras nodded toward the camp. "I see you've been fairly successful gathering the knights."

"All but one," Quinlan said. "But we're ready."

"That's why I'm here," Taras said. "You have a mission."

This was what Quinlan was waiting for. He knew Burkfield was a focal point for Lucius, and he was eager to see how the Swords of Valor could contribute to its rescue and restoration.

"What's the mission?" he asked eagerly.

Taras gave a businesslike nod. "You and the other Swords of Valor are to escort a shipment of swords that are arriving from Cameria and being delivered to Chessington. From there they will be delivered to havens throughout the kingdom."

Quinlan stared at Taras, not believing what he heard.

Taras continued. "Your escort point begins at Whighton, and you must be there in four days."

"But what of Burkfield?" Quinlan asked. "I thought that all this time I was being trained so the Swords of Valor could defend Burkfield."

Taras crossed his arms in his usual commanding way.

"We're not fighting a battle, Quinlan. We're fighting a war. Burkfield has been a battle zone between our forces for a long time. Why do you think Baylor and the Swords of Valor were there when they found you? We have committed thousands of Silent Warriors to defending the city. But the fact is, when the Knights of the Prince quit caring, they and the whole city became vulnerable to Lucius's attacks, and there is very little we can do about it now. It is almost impossible to recover a city once it reaches this point. Only the Prince Himself could bring it back now."

"But we could—"

"I'm sorry, Quinlan. Sometimes you have to lose a battle to win the war, and that's what we're facing here."

Quinlan stared up at the huge warrior as he thought of Tav, his family, and especially of Sir Edmund.

"Sir Edmund cares," he said, "and I made a commitment to him. There are others who care too. They just need help, and I know how to help them."

Taras looked sternly at Quinlan and was about to speak, but Quinlan continued.

"Please, Taras, let me try. Burkfield can be saved, and I know in my heart that the Prince has called me there."

At that, Taras hesitated. He turned and walked away a few paces, then turned back and stared at Quinlan. "Sir Edmund is a good man, but it takes more than one to save a city. Burkfield is so far gone now it would take thousands."

Quinlan's heart began to sink.

Taras shook his head as if in regret. "I can't promise support from the Silent Warriors. Our missions lie elsewhere now."

Quinlan's eyes opened wide. He closed the few paces between them. "Thank you, Taras." Quinlan reached out his arm, and Taras took it.

"You have four weeks," the Silent Warrior said, "no more." Then he disappeared as quietly as he had come.

Quinlan stood there a long time, staring after his mysterious friend. The world of the warriors slowly drifted away as he set his course and mind to the world of men and women. Though he had trained in both worlds, his heart had always remained right where the Prince had found him…in Arrethtrae. This was his battle, even if he had to fight it alone.

When he arrived back with his knights, they knew in an instant that something had changed.

"What is it, Commander?" Kessler asked.

Quinlan drew a deep breath. "Fellow knights, from the lips of Lucius's own lieutenants I heard that Burkfield's destruction is an integral part of the Dark Lord's plan to take over the kingdom. I cannot stand by and watch that happen. I will fight beside Sir Edmund for the haven, the people…and the children." Quinlan glanced at Drake. "But I have just learned the Silent Warriors might not be available to support us in this mission, so it may well be a futile fight."

He gazed around at his assembled colleagues. "You are all free to go—without shame."

Silence hung in the air a long minute. Then Lilam drew her sword. "I'm with you, Commander."

"And I," Kessler and Drake said together and drew their swords.

Just then a horse galloped up behind them and stopped in a wash of dirt and wind.

"I don't know what we're voting for," Purcell said, reaching for his sword, "but count me in." He looked at Lilam and smiled. "Finally… someone prettier than I in this ragged unit."

Lilam rolled her eyes while Quinlan exchanged a nod with Purcell. Then he drew his own sword. "Remember who you serve, Knights of the Prince."

They brought their swords together.

"Swords of Valor for Him," they said in unison.

The next morning, the unit rode together to the nearest main road. Quinlan sent Drake, Kessler, and Purcell in three different directions, with orders to meet back in Burkfield in ten days. Then he and Lilam set their course for Thecia, a three-day journey to the northeast. There, Quinlan hoped to meet with a man with whom he had a common friend…and a common enemy.

The haven at Thecia was large and bustling. Quinlan and Lilam followed directions to a building across a busy courtyard. Once inside the door, however, they were halted by the same young woman Quinlan had bumped into in Burkfield the year before. His face burned as he requested an audience with Sir Worthington.

"Sir Worthington is preparing for a mission and can't be disturbed."

"Will you give him a message then while I wait?" Quinlan said.

"I'll give him the message, but it won't do you any good to wait… Do I know you?" The woman leaned closer and stared at Quinlan with narrowed eyes.

Quinlan took a step back, once again unnerved by her presence. She was just too pretty, too blunt…and way too close.

"No, you don't," Quinlan said quickly. "Listen, I have an urgent message, and I really need to see—"

"I remember you from Burkfield!" she exclaimed, quite pleased with herself.

Great, Quinlan thought. *Now she'll never let me see him.*

"Raisa?" An inner door opened, and Worthington looked out.

The woman spun about. "Yes, brother."

Brother? Quinlan looked back at the woman.

Worthington stopped and opened the door fully when he saw Quinlan. His eyes widened. "You're the man from Arimil." He held out his hand. "That was one of the most terrifying experiences of my life, and I'll never forget the men who saved me."

Raisa raised her eyebrows. "I don't think you've got the right man, brother. This is the one—"

"You're welcome, sir." Quinlan grabbed the hand while simultaneously putting his left hand on Worthington's shoulder and walking him back toward his chamber. "Sir, there is a dire situation I need to talk to you about."

Several hours later, Quinlan finally emerged from Worthington's chamber. Lilam sat in a chair across the room from Raisa with her arms crossed. Quinlan nodded for her to follow him, hoping she wasn't too upset about being abandoned. Raisa glared at Quinlan as he passed.

"Thank you, miss." He tilted his head to her. "And by the way, I was brave enough to come back after all."

Raisa opened her mouth to say something, but Quinlan and Lilam were out the door before she had a chance.

"I don't like that woman," Lilam groused as they crossed the courtyard toward their horses.

Quinlan laughed. "I know what you mean... I don't much like her either."

"So," Lilam asked, "were you successful?"

Quinlan shrugged. "We shall see."

"Where to now?"

"To start a battle!"

Quinlan and Lilam arrived back in Burkfield three days later and waited for Kessler, Drake, and Purcell to return. He and Lilam put those four days to good use conducting extensive reconnaissance on the city and the surrounding area. He even met with the prefect of Burkfield to warn him of the impending battle, but it didn't go well.

"Your warning is preposterous," the stocky, gray-haired man said. "And you'd better not make a stir in my city, or you'll be asked to leave!"

Quinlan looked at the prefect and realized he was asking a blind man to see the colors of a rainbow.

"There will not be a stir in your city, sir," he said soberly. "It will be a battle—one that you cannot stop. I am committed to fighting for the city and her people. All I'm asking for is your cooperation."

The prefect huffed. "We are a city at peace with all orders in the kingdom. I will not disrupt our lives because of some wild-eyed warning."

Quinlan stared at the prefect for a moment. "Thank you for your time, sir." He turned to leave, but stopped at the door and looked back. "In truth, sir, there are only two real orders in the kingdom. One is coming to destroy you. The other will try to save you. At some point, everyone must choose to which one they will belong."

Quinlan left the prefect's chamber wondering if it was even possible to save someone who could not see he needed to be saved.

In the evening of the following day, Quinlan made a secret visit to a shop on a merchant street just off the main thoroughfare. All the shops had closed except one. Quinlan waited in the shadows until the back door opened and the bald, whistling shop owner stepped out.

"You're a busy man," Quinlan said.

The man turned with a start. "Who goes there?"

Quinlan stepped into the light that shone from the door. "My name is Quinlan, and I'm a very dissatisfied customer."

"Ha! Do you think I really care?" The man's voice changed from that of a perky, whistling merchant to something dark and threatening.

Quinlan grabbed him by the collar and shoved him up against the back of the shop, not caring that the man was larger than he. "You'd better care," Quinlan growled, just inches from his face. "Because if you don't, you'll die early."

"You have no idea who you're dealing with, Knight of the Prince." The man's eyes practically glowed with hatred.

"I don't?—Pathyon, pawn of Lucius!"

The Shadow Warrior smiled. He moved just slightly, and Quinlan suddenly felt a knife press into his side.

"I've spent the last two years killing fools of the Prince like you. What makes you think you're so different, my ignorant little—"

Four brilliant swords appeared out of the dark and came to rest with their tips against the Shadow Warrior's neck.

"Because we're here with him," Drake said.

Pathyon's smile evaporated. He lowered the knife and lifted his chin to keep his blood from spilling.

Quinlan jerked his forearm away from the warrior's chest. "You have five days to rid the entire city of your paythas and leave. If you don't, you'll not live to day six."

The Swords of Valor released Pathyon, and he slipped away into the night.

"He'll never do it," Lilam said.

"Of course not," Quinlan replied.

"Then why didn't we just kill him and be rid of him?" Purcell asked.

"Because he's just a little fish carrying a message for us." Quinlan took a deep breath. "And I think it worked."

TWENTY-TWO

A ROARING LION

"There's trouble, my lord." Luskan spoke with great hesitation.

Lucius looked up furiously from his intricately carved throne. "What did you say?"

"Lord Pathyon has reported that a Knight of the Prince named Sir Quinlan has resurrected the Swords of Valor, and they are in Burkfield. I think—"

"Burkfield!" Lucius screamed and rose up out of his chair. "I don't hear about this until they are all the way to Burkfield?"

Lucius clenched his jaw and wrapped his powerful fingers around his sword. Luskan cringed and took a step backward.

"Destroy the city now!" Lucius commanded with a fist in Luskan's face. "See to it personally, Luskan, and do not fail me. Take two legions of Shadow Warriors *and* your Assassins. Decimate Burkfield, and I want all of the Swords of Valor dead—do you hear me? Dead!"

TWENTY-THREE

THE BATTLE FOR BURKFIELD

Quinlan let out a low whistle as he stood on Mount Resolute and scanned the countryside surrounding Burkfield. Like a collapsing circle of phosphorescent green, the Shadow Warriors came—thousands of them. They were still at least two hours away. That should give Quinlan and the Swords of Valor just enough time.

Quinlan lowered the crystal coin and swallowed. "They got the message."

"Let me see that," Purcell grabbed for the crystal coin. He looked in all directions. "I don't see a thing."

Kessler laughed and slapped Purcell on the back. "That's why he's commander, chum."

"How many?" Drake asked.

Quinlan hesitated. "Difficult to say. Many thousands."

The five knights looked at Quinlan soberly, fully understanding the implications. At that moment, Quinlan understood Baylor's words about feeling responsible for his comrades' lives. The trust in their eyes made the burden all the heavier.

He drew his sword and they followed suit. "Remember who you serve, Knights of the Prince," he said as he placed his sword in the middle of their circle.

"Swords of Valor for Him!" they chorused.

"It's time to move," Quinlan commanded. "Sir Edmund has gathered any Knights of the Prince left in the city to the haven, so we'll start there. We must take care of the paythas first; then we'll worry about the Shadow Warriors."

They mounted up and galloped toward the haven. Before entering, Quinlan gathered the four together.

"Do not attempt to kill a paytha unless its host allows it…or you may end up killing the knight."

The other knights looked at him in disbelief.

"They're vicious," he insisted. "Get ready."

Sir Edmund had gathered forty-three knights in the main training arena, all with very agitated paythas on their shoulders. More than half of the knights no longer even carried swords. Quinlan was glad to see Tav among them. His old friend smiled broadly and walked toward Quinlan, but Quinlan held up a hand to stop him.

"Knights of the Prince"—he shouted to get their attention—"Burkfield is under siege and soon will be attacked by a large force of Shadow Warriors."

The knights fell silent. Two of the paythas began to growl.

"The paythas on your backs are part of Lucius's plan to destroy you and this city. If you want to survive, you must be rid of them."

At that there was a stir among the knights. More of the paythas growled, and their hosts could hardly keep them under control. Quinlan could tell that his comrades were surprised by the rising intensity of the situation.

One of the female knights had a paytha on her back that was so large she could hardly carry it anymore. She stepped forward and the beast growled, sinking its claws deep into her shoulders and back.

"Please take it away," she cried, falling to the ground.

Drake and Kessler moved closer, but the paytha snarled and bared its teeth. The knight screamed as it clung more tightly to her. One little arm wrapped itself around her neck, ready to tear into her with its claws.

Purcell stepped up behind Drake and pulled his knife. Kessler diverted the creature's attention by coming close to it on the opposite side. Purcell timed his throw perfectly. As the animal swiped at Kessler, the knife sank deep behind its outstretched arm and into its heart. The beast let out one loud cry and went limp.

Lilam and Kessler ran to the knight and pulled the slain beast from her back. They helped her to her feet and pulled her away from the others knights, who looked on in horror. The paythas were now in a complete state of agitation and fury.

"These creatures are straight from Lucius," Quinlan said to them. "We will help you."

At that, some of the knights ran for the gate. Some stayed and fell to the ground pleading for help, while others seemed frozen in indecision. Sir Edmund and the Swords of Valor began helping those who asked for help. The smaller paythas proved easy to dislodge and kill, but others proved very painful for their hosts.

In the midst of the confusion, Tav ran over to Quinlan. "What are you doing?"

"Tav, that beast is evil." Quinlan pointed at Disty, who snarled viciously from Tav's shoulder. "Let me help you," Quinlan urged. "We need you in the battle that's coming."

Tav took a backward step. "Stay away." He turned and ran toward the gate. Grabbing Valiant's reins, he mounted and rode back toward Burkfield at breakneck speed, while Quinlan stared sadly after him.

By the time it was over, they had recovered eighteen knights. Sir Edmund issued swords for those without them, and Quinlan led a force of twenty-four knights into Burkfield.

It was market day, and the city seemed unusually full of activity and people, almost as if a citywide festival were about to begin. Every shop on every street seemed crowded with eager customers. Quinlan told Edmund to gather his knights at the bell tower and wait for his signal; then he led the Swords of Valor farther down the main thoroughfare.

As they rode, snarling paythas began to appear from behind shops and alleyways. The entire city seemed infested with the beasts. The alarmed townspeople stepped aside and away as fast as they could. Then

Pathyon emerged from the street his shop was on, surrounded by hundreds of paythas. As he walked down the center of the main thoroughfare with his army of paythas, the people cleared off the street, staring in wonder at what was happening.

"This isn't the kind of enemy I planned on fighting today," Purcell muttered as the five of them tried to keep their steeds under control. They all drew their swords.

"What of the Shadow Warriors?" Drake asked.

"Don't worry," Quinlan said. "They're on their way."

"That's not exactly what I meant," Drake said as the paythas began to close in.

Pathyon walked to within thirty paces of the unit and stopped, stroking the paytha in his arms. "There are those in both worlds who think me just an insignificant vice," he said. "But as you can see, I rule this city—more completely than any other lord rules any other city. You are the fool after all, Knight of the Prince."

Pathyon whispered to the creature he was holding. It bared its teeth at Quinlan and his knights, then jumped from his arms and began running toward them. Hundreds of others followed.

"And our plan is what again?" Purcell asked with a smirk as the paythas closed in.

Quinlan put his fingers to his mouth and whistled. A strange sound erupted from the near side of the city's edge, and all the paythas stopped. The silence was broken only by the thumping sound of a flatfooted beast romping down the cobblestoned street. Suddenly, from an alleyway off to the right, Kalil burst forth with an echoing trumpet sound. Screams and alarms rose up from the people as the powerful animal raised its five trunks in the air and crouched as if to spring.

Drake, Kessler, and Purcell readied their swords.

"Hold, men," Quinlan said. "This one's our friend."

"You're kidding," Purcell said. "That is the ugliest beast I've ever seen."

"Mind your words, Purcell," Lilam said with a smile. "He's sensitive—and well trained."

Purcell shot an utterly perplexed look at Lilam as Quinlan motioned to Kalil. The penthomoth charged into the hundreds of paythas with a fury. They tried to retaliate but couldn't penetrate the animal's tough hide. The five trunks made short work of any paytha that came within its reach, crushing and discarding them like flawed water flasks. They kept coming at him in relentless waves, but Kalil trampled, squeezed, and threw paythas every which way. Finally the few remaining began running away, but Kalil charged after them, killing any that he saw.

When it was over, Pathyon stood alone. He cursed the Swords of Valor, drew his sword, and ran back toward his shop.

Quinlan ignored him. He looked to the eastern hills surrounding the city and closed his eyes, then turned to the west. The collapsing circle of green was now much more concentrated and nearly upon them.

"Give the signal, Drake!" Quinlan commanded.

Drake attached the flag of the Knights of the Prince to the end of his sword and raised it high for Sir Edmund to see at the bell tower. A moment later the bells of the tower began to ring. In an instant the city of Burkfield was transformed. The people in the streets began drawing swords from wagons, barrels, clothing, and any other place capable of hiding a sword—thousands upon thousands, all bearing the mark of the Prince.

Worthington had done his job well, as had Kessler, Drake, and Purcell. The Knights of the Prince had come from across the kingdom to fight against the minions of Lucius on behalf of Burkfield. Chills ran up and down Quinlan's spine as he witnessed the courage of fellow Followers unveiled.

"Ironic, isn't it?" Kessler said with a smile. "All these years we've been the secret Swords of Valor defending them. Now they are the secret Swords of Valor defending us."

Quinlan turned as Sir Worthington and Lady Raisa galloped up to the valor knights and reined in their steeds.

"Your orders, Commander?" Worthington said. Raisa stared at Quinlan with fresh respect.

"They know we know." Quinlan gazed toward the hills. "Set up the perimeter defenses. We have but a few moments. According to our re-connaissance, there are three Shadow Warriors yet in the city—Pathyon and two others. We will find them, but tell your men to be wary. There may be Vincero Knights as well."

Worthington saluted and galloped off to command his knights. Quinlan turned to his comrades. "We must find these Shadow Warriors quickly. The devastation they wreak from within could turn the course of the battle."

He led them at a gallop toward the street where Pathyon's shop stood, then stopped and scanned left and right.

"Drake, Purcell—the cooper's shop." They dismounted and ran to the corner building that had barrels stacked outside. Quinlan led Kessler and Lilam to Pathyon's shop, but it was empty, and their fruitless hunt was taking valuable time. Already, from the edges of the city, Quinlan could hear the sounds of battle.

Quinlan grew uneasy, wanting to join with Worthington in the defense of Burkfield but knowing the devastation three Shadow Warriors could do from within. He scanned the shop again—nothing. Then he scanned the opposite side of the street. At the back left corner of the shop across the street, Quinlan caught an almost imperceptible glimmer of green.

"There!" he whispered to Kessler and Lilam.

The shop was one of three in a larger building. Quinlan sent Kessler and Lilam around the right side of the building while he took the left. He had almost reached the back corner when he heard a boot scrape on wood up above. He looked up just in time to see Pathyon falling on top of him from the roof, his blade protruding like a spear.

Quinlan deflected Pathyon's blade with a high horizontal crosscut, but the crash of bodies and armor splayed both combatants out com-pletely and dislodged their swords from their grips. Quinlan took the brunt of the fall, and Pathyon was on him in an instant. The warrior's left hand encircled Quinlan's throat as he pounded a gauntleted fist into his face. Fighting unconsciousness, Quinlan deflected the blows.

Pathyon drew Quinlan's knife from its sheath to use against him, but Quinlan swung his right arm inside Pathyon's left arm and gained enough leverage to break the grip on his neck. Pathyon thrust with the knife, but Quinlan caught his hand at the last moment and kicked the warrior off him. As he scrambled to his feet, he heard the clash of swords on the far end of the building. Kessler and Lilam were engaged as well, and he could not count on any help from them.

"You might as well give up," Pathyon sneered. "You've lost this city already!" Then he lunged at Quinlan, thrusting the knife in front of him. Quinlan was grateful for Zeke's training, for he knew exactly what to do.

He retreated one step to allow the plunge to expire, then grabbed Pathyon's right wrist with his left hand. He swung the warrior's arm up into the air, stepped through and underneath it, then pivoted around, placing his right arm in the crux of Pathyon's right elbow joint. He was now in complete control of the knife and the arm that held it. In one quick motion he pulled the knife into Pathyon's chest. Pathyon dropped to his knees and fell against the wall of the nearby building while Quinlan searched for his sword.

The sounds of desperate fighting at the edges of the city told Quinlan that the battle had now fully matured. He heard hoofs on the cobblestones and turned to see a mounted knight in the street—Raisa. She looked as if she had already faced a dozen Shadow Warriors.

"Sir Worthington asked me to find you." Her voice cracked with worry. "The eastern perimeter is failing, and the south is weak. There are too many."

"Tell Worthington we're coming," Quinlan said.

Hope sparked in Raisa's eyes, and she kicked her steed back down the street.

Quinlan reached down to grab his sword but then froze, sensing something dark nearby. Deep laughter reverberated off the walls and rattled him. Quinlan stood and turned to see a warrior whose stature made Pathyon look like a boy. It was a warrior he'd seen once before and never wanted to see again.

"It's hopeless, knave," said Luskan. "Two legions of Lucius's most powerful Shadow Warriors are impossible to stop. Even those pathetic Silent Warriors can't help you now...*if* they wanted to!"

Luskan threw his head back and reveled in contemptuous laughter. When he was through, he glared at Quinlan and strode toward him with his sword drawn, passing by Pathyon, who was still huddled by the wall.

"Luskan...," Pathyon wheezed and held up a hand.

Luskan stopped. "You pitiful excuse for a warrior." With one quick thrust he pierced Pathyon through, then kicked him with his boot to withdraw his sword. As Pathyon fell dead, Luskan turned toward Quinlan, the gleam of bloodlust in his eyes.

Quinlan held his sword before him and backed up into the street as the evil commander slowly moved toward him.

He chanced a quick glance toward the end of the building where Kessler and Lilam had been engaged and saw them also backing up into the street. The look on their faces said something ghastly was coming at them too.

Once clear, they ran to join Quinlan just as Drake and Purcell came running from the left.

The five valor knights now stood together in the street...and destruction was closing in. ▨

TWENTY-FOUR

SWORDS OF VALOR

"Remember I said there are warriors you never want to face?" Kessler whispered as Luskan entered the street from the side of the building. "This is one of them."

And Luskan wasn't alone. Fifteen warriors with black and green painted faces emerged from both sides of the building—the same warriors that had attacked Garriston and killed Sir Baylor.

"I thought you said there were only three Shadow Warriors in the city," Lilam said.

Quinlan briefly closed his eyes, but all he saw was Luskan's green glow.

"I can't see the painted ones," he said, confused. Then, with a jolt, he realized Baylor hadn't been able to see them either.

The paint, the tightly fitting armor, the black bands across the eyes somehow hid these warriors from the lens of the kasilite medallion. That's why Baylor had signaled only four Shadow Warriors when there had actually been six—and that's why he had died. Even if Quinlan had been at his post, the outcome wouldn't have changed.

Relief flooded over Quinlan, then vanished as he remembered his fight with one of these painted warriors. He and his colleagues were badly outnumbered, but even if the numbers had been even, their chances of victory against these warriors would be slim.

Quinlan opened his mouth to order a retreat. Then he looked around and saw ten more painted warriors come up behind them.

"Finally!" Luskan's low, un-Arrethtraen voice seemed to bounce off the buildings. "My Assassin Warriors have trapped the infamous Swords of Valor."

Surrounded, the valor knights formed a tight circle with their backs to one another in the center of the street. The Assassin Warriors quickly surrounded them. All seemed lost—their lives, and the city itself—for now they would never be able to help Worthington in time.

"The painted warriors are different," Quinlan warned his comrades. "Your first thrust must be fatal, or they will rise again."

"Now, that's an important safety tip," Kessler quipped.

"I swear, Kessler," Purcell scoffed, "you really don't know when to quit being funny."

"If these Assassin Warriors get to the knights protecting the city—," Quinlan began.

"They won't," Drake said with vehemence.

"Let's take them." Lilam swung her sword in anticipation of the fight.

"Killing all of you will be almost as sweet as killing Baylor," Luskan taunted.

"Remember who you serve, knights," Quinlan said. "The King reigns!"

"And His Son!" they shouted in unison.

"Kill them!" Luskan ordered.

The first line of Assassin Warriors lunged into the wall of defensive swords wielded by the valor knights. The unit worked with flawless teamwork. Lilam advanced, and Drake covered her side. Quinlan felled one warrior, then blasted the sword of Purcell's opponent aside so that Purcell could complete a perfect thrust and put that warrior down. Kessler feigned retreat while Drake diverted a slice that cut clean through the torso of Kessler's opponent. Then Kessler assumed Drake's fight while Quinlan covered for Lilam.

Minute by minute the fight continued, the clash of swords and daggers ringing in the street. The Assassin Warriors fought viciously and without emotion, as if their only purpose in life was to kill and be killed. Many an Assassin Warrior rose up after a valor knight thought him dead, but many others fell, never to rise again. Still the fight continued.

A roar of fury rose over the sounds of battle as Luskan realized his Assassins were not overcoming the valor knights. Enraged, he strode toward the fray, sword swinging. Quinlan's heart sank, and he opened his mouth to warn his comrades.

"Luskan!" The fight paused as all eyes turned in the direction of the powerful voice.

There, like a bastion of kingly power, stood Taras. Both swords protruded from his back scabbards, waiting to be used. He withdrew them both and pointed to opposite sides of the city. "We have come to help those who belong to the Prince!"

Quinlan looked to the hills and saw a ribbon of violet light descending quickly.

"And *I*"—Taras pointed both swords at Luskan—"have come for *you*!"

He swirled both swords in anticipation of the fight. Luskan growled, and the two warriors ran toward each other in an epic clash of dark and light.

"*Thusia!*" At this cryptic command from Luskan, the Assassin Warriors renewed their attack with suicidal vengeance. The tide of the battle turned as the valor knights began to falter.

Purcell took a slice across his leg and fell to one knee, and Quinlan barely managed to deflect the deathblow that followed. Quinlan heard Lilam gasp and turned to see an Assassin withdraw a sword from her shoulder. Purcell's hastily thrown knife found its mark in that Shadow Warrior's neck, but another Assassin stepped in to take his place.

Quinlan felt defeat crashing down upon them. He glanced at Taras, who was locked in an intense duel with Luskan. Then he saw something scurry across the street and realized he still had one strategic maneuver left.

He whistled loudly and heard Kalil's trumpet reply. The penthomoth burst onto the street with paythas screaming in three of his trunks. He smashed them into the nearest wall, then looked toward the valor knights.

Quinlan didn't need to signal. The animal charged the Assassins from behind with the full rage of a protective beast. Kalil's appearance renewed hope, and the tide turned once more. The valor knights' swords flew swiftly as Kalil trampled, crushed, and threw Assassins every which way.

Within moments the fight was over. Quinlan ordered Kessler to tend to Lilam and Drake to Purcell. At that moment, a cheer rose from the city's northern border. It seemed to flow around them like a wave.

Quinlan looked for Taras. His fight had ended too, and he was walking toward them. Quinlan saw Luskan mounted and riding away, cradling his arm. The battle for Burkfield was over, and the Knights of the Prince stood victorious.

Quinlan took a few steps toward Taras, who was still fifteen paces away, but the look on the face of this mighty warrior confused him.

"Watch out!" Taras yelled and pointed behind Quinlan. Quinlan turned to see that a wounded Assassin Warrior had risen up and was in the last few degrees of a deadly arc aimed right for Quinlan's back.

There was no time to react. It was over. But the air split open with a trumpet call, and at the final fraction of a second before the warrior's blade would have split Quinlan in two, Kalil lunged into the warrior and crushed him beneath his powerful legs. The attack had a cost, however, and the penthomoth tumbled to the ground with the warrior's blade plunged deep into its side.

"No!" Quinlan ran to his friend.

Kalil bellowed as Quinlan removed the sword, and the animal tried in vain to rise. Finally he slumped to the ground, crying in pain.

Quinlan fell on the animal's neck as Taras and the Swords of Valor gathered around. "You've given too much, my friend," he said through tears.

Kalil lifted his central trunk and stroked Quinlan's shoulder as if to say, "It's all right. That's why I came with you."

Kalil's breathing became shallow, and his trunk slowly fell from

Quinlan's shoulder. Then he grew still, and Quinlan mourned the loss of another great friend.

Lilam knelt and put a hand on Quinlan's shoulder. "I'm so sorry, Quinlan. Only the noble in heart can give such a sacrifice."

Kessler added his hand to Lilam's. "All of us owe him our—"

The clatter of hoofs on cobblestone interrupted. Sir Worthington, Lady Raisa, Sir Edmund, and four other knights approached on horseback. Quinlan stood, knowing a commander's grief must often be postponed. In the dark of night he would return to his grief in honor of his fallen friend.

"What is your status, Sir Worthington?" Quinlan asked.

"There are many wounded," Worthington replied, "but they are being cared for. The Silent Warriors came just in time or the situation would have been much worse."

Quinlan turned to thank Taras for his last-minute aid, but the Silent Warrior was gone. Quinlan had a feeling he would see him again before too long.

He turned back and offered Worthington his hand. "Thank you for all you've done." Worthington gripped his forearm tightly, and Quinlan knew a lifelong friendship had been forged that day. Worthington turned to Edmund and began talking about rebuilding the haven, while the other knights discussed the events of the battle.

"Sir Quinlan," a soft voice called. Quinlan turned to see Lady Raisa step toward him. He wondered what awkwardness or insult he might suffer this time.

She gave him a sheepish smile instead. "I believe I may owe you an apology...or two."

Quinlan thought of their encounters and realized her actions may not have been ill-intended. After all, had it not been for Raisa, he might never have left Burkfield to find the Prince.

"Actually, Raisa," he said, "you were the only one who saw my struggle and was brave enough to address it."

"I don't have my brother's gift with words." She glanced toward Worthington. "Sometimes my zeal for the Prince and my tongue get me in trouble. I'm truly sorry."

Quinlan smiled at her. "Your words stung, but they were true. Speaking the hard truth is often the best thing you can do for a friend."

Raisa looked at him with a gleam in her eye and slowly shook her head. "I sensed then that there was more to you. I just didn't realize how much more."

Quinlan looked away, embarrassed by her penetrating gaze. An awkward silence followed; then Raisa put her hand on Quinlan's arm.

"I'm grateful for your kind words, Sir Quinlan." She turned to mount her horse.

"Lady Raisa," Quinlan called to her, and she spun about.

"Yes?"

"Thank you for what you and your brother have done here today."

"It is our duty...to help a friend," she said. "You're welcome."

"Perhaps when I pass through Thecia we could talk again."

"I would like that very much." She flashed him a warm smile, then mounted up and rode off with Worthington to help in the recovery.

Quinlan turned to check on his unit, but his gaze fell first upon a man kneeling near the corner of one of the shops. He was looking at the dead paythas strewn about, but a very large live one still rode on his shoulder. Tav turned toward Quinlan, and their eyes locked. Quinlan beckoned to him, but Tav just stood and walked away, the sword of the Prince hanging idle at his side. Quinlan's heart wrenched for his friend who had been a brother, but Sir Baylor's words rang in his ears: "Everyone must choose for himself."

Quinlan sighed and walked to check on Purcell and Lilam. Their wounds were significant but not life threatening. If all went well, they would recover fully.

"That was quite the first mission." Purcell pushed up on his elbows and flashed a crooked grin. "I don't think *any* mission with you is going to be boring...Commander."

Kessler, Drake, and Lilam laughed in agreement. Quinlan smiled and shook his head. He knew they were right...but he also knew it wasn't he who brought such adventure. It was the journey of following the Prince that did so—a journey he couldn't wait to continue.

THE WAY OF THE WISE, THE WAY OF A FOOL

 In the years before the Rising, a time when Lucius gained control of all Arrethtrae and ruled in tyranny, Quinlan led the Swords of Valor on many great missions for the Prince. The life he lived did indeed reverberate across the kingdom, saving many from the clutches of the Dark Knight and bringing many to the Prince.

Unfortunately, this story of two knights, Sir Quinlan and Sir Gustav, does not end there. The day the Prince came for His faithful knights was a day of great joy…and of great sorrow. The grand ships arrived to take the Knights of the Prince home, and I, Cedric, was aboard the ship when Sir Quinlan came to the dock where the Prince stood. Quinlan fell to his knees before the mighty One, and the Prince lifted him up.

"Well done, my good and faithful knight," the Prince said with joy in his voice. Quinlan was received and entered the ship with gladness.

Then, as we were about to embark, Sir Gustav—Quinlan's friend Tav—came running for the docks. His paytha, snarling and growling, dug its claws into Gustav's shoulders, but he came anyway. As he approached the docks, however, the paytha could not take being in the presence of the Prince. It jumped from Gustav's shoulder and fell into the sea.

"I am here, my Prince. I am here!" Tav cried with hope in his eyes, but the Prince held up His hand and would not let him come.

Gustav knelt down and pleaded, "But I wore your mark and carried the sword of the King with me everywhere."

The Prince looked sadly at Sir Gustav. "You made for yourself a life of selfish and apathetic comfort in this kingdom. Sir Quinlan chose to make his life in the Kingdom Across the Sea. That is where each of you built. That is where each of you will live. Depart from Me, for I never knew you."

Quinlan's heart broke for his friend, but the judgment had been given. Tav turned away and returned to that place where he had stored up his treasures…treasures that had no worth to a King who owned everything.

And thus you have heard the tale of two knights—the way of the wise and the way of a fool. Both had defining moments, and both made their choices.

Perhaps your defining moment is upon *you*. I implore you, my fellow knight—choose wisely!

DISCUSSION QUESTIONS

Much of the allegorical symbolism in the Knights of Arrethtrae originated in the Kingdom Series. Here are a few questions to review this symbolism:

1. Who does the Prince represent?
2. Who are the Knights of the Prince?
3. What is Chessington? Arrethtrae?
4. Who is the Dark Knight/Dark Lord/Lucius?
5. Who are the Silent Warriors and the Shadow Warriors?
6. What is a Vincero Knight?
7. What is a haven?

Questions for *Sir Quinlan and the Swords of Valor*

CHAPTER 1
1. In this chapter, the Dark Knight, Lucius, is searching for a particular effective form of attack against the citizens of Arrethtrae. When is evil the most dangerous to us?

CHAPTER 2
1. What do you think the paytha creature might represent?
2. When Twitch asks the merchant how big the paytha will get, the answer is "as big as you want it." How does this strange characteristic relate to the symbolism of the creature?
3. How does the merchant's offer to trade for weapons or armor relate to a compromise in our spiritual walk to gain something worldly?
4. What does the shield represent in Ephesians 6:16? How does this relate to what Tav might be giving up by trading his shield to gain the paytha?

CHAPTER 3

1. Tav and Twitch name their paythas Disty and Bli. What do these names represent in regard to apathy?

2. The merchant explains that paythas can reproduce if they are fed and cared for and if they sense that others are enjoying them too. How does this relate to apathy?

CHAPTER 4

1. Sir Baylor states that following the Prince requires sacrifice. Can you find a Bible verse to support this point of view?

CHAPTER 5

1. Why do you think Bli becomes distressed when Quinlan kneels down to speak to the Prince? How does this relate to the spiritual realm?

2. Why does a Shadow Warrior attack Quinlan?

3. As the Swords of Valor fight to protect Quinlan, he notices that as individuals they would have quickly fallen, but as a force of four, they form an "impenetrable wall." Can you find a Bible verse supporting how this is true for us as the body of Christ?

CHAPTER 6

1. No one seems to believe that Quinlan is worthy of being a knight who can serve with the Swords of Valor. Does this relate to the kinds of people God often calls to service for Him? Can you think of examples in the Bible? Why do you think God works this way?

2. What do the Articles of the Code and the Sword of the Prince represent?

3. Sir Baylor remarks, "Those knights who are truly dedicated to the Prince see the true kingdom well, but those who are not—and there are many—do not see it at all." Can this be true of Christians? If so, what might cause this?

4. Sir Baylor speaks of supporting those knights who have purposed to take the message of the Prince into the far reaches of the kingdom. How can you support missionaries today?

5. Quinlan resolves to follow the prompting within him to serve the Prince by joining the Swords of Valor. Can you find Bible verses that tell us not to shrink back or quench the promptings of the Holy Spirit?

CHAPTER 7

1. Quinlan overhears a visiting knight at the haven teaching her trainees that the sword is "our greatest defense against the forces of evil." Why is this true? How can we use the sword of God's Word as a defense? Can you think of a biblical example of this?

CHAPTER 8

1. After the attack at the haven, a knight wonders if some of the people might ask where the Prince was in all of it. Often we are faced with the same question in real life. What is a good answer for someone who wonders where God is in the tragedies of the world?

CHAPTER 9

1. In an empire built on deception and treachery (such as the realm of Lucius), there are no friends. Why do you think this is?

CHAPTER 10

1. Sir Worthington urges the knights that "when your heart pounds with passion" for the cause of the Prince, "you take up a battle that has been raging from the beginning of time." Do you really believe this statement? If so, how does it affect how you live your daily life?

CHAPTER 11

1. We see Tav's apathy turn to unbelief when he says Quinlan is chasing a dream that doesn't exist. How does this happen to a believer? Find Bible verses to support your answer.

2. Terrance encourages Quinlan to quit looking back at his past so that he won't stumble over the things that are ahead of him. Find a passage in Philippians that teaches us to look forward.

CHAPTER 12

1. By using the crystal coin, Quinlan discovers that he can see in the warrior realm. What allows us to "see" the spiritual realm?

CHAPTER 13

1. Part of Quinlan's training involves strengthening his body by first tearing it down, then building it back up. Can you think of a discipline in Scripture that requires us to deny our bodies in order for us to become stronger *spiritually*?

2. As Taras instructs Quinlan, he makes three statements about Quinlan's identity as a Knight of the Prince. The first is, "The Prince sees you not for who you think you are, but for who He knows you are. The truth is that when He died for you on that tree long ago and when you accepted Him as the Son of the King, you already became that which you hope you will become." Can you think of Bible verses that state a similar reality? What does this mean for us today?

3. The second statement Taras makes about Quinlan's identity is: "Most of the knights don't even understand who they are in the Prince." How do we as Christians find out who we are in Christ?

4. The final statement Taras makes about Quinlan's identity is: "You cannot add anything to that which the Prince made perfect. All you can do is believe Him who made it so." In other words, Christ's work on the cross was complete, and we can't add anything to it to help sanctify ourselves. Our righteous-

ness is based not on what we do, but on our believing Jesus
Christ and what He did for us. Which book of the New
Testament shows how faith in God was attributed to people
as righteousness?

CHAPTER 14

1. In this chapter Luskan speaks of "the Rising," which was
   also mentioned in chapter 1. What do you think this might
   represent?

CHAPTER 15

1. "It's what I was born to be." Lilam's statement about becoming
   a Knight of the Prince is really true for all people of the world.
   Why? Find a scripture to support your answer.

CHAPTERS 16 AND 17

1. Note how the paythas, which represent apathy, appeared
   friendly at first and later were revealed to be vicious, controlling
   beasts, whereas Kalil the penthomoth first appeared vicious, but
   later becomes a friend. What do you think the penthomoth
   represents? (The Greek work *pentho* provides a hint.)
2. Kalil the penthomoth becomes a friend to Quinlan, but not
   every penthomoth is a friend. What does this tell us?

CHAPTER 18

1. As Quinlan searches for the warrior hiding in the forest, he
   realizes that he has been depending on the training from the
   Silent Warriors and has completely forgotten about the crystal
   coin. Often we forget to access the power of the Holy Spirit
   and depend instead on our own wisdom and ability. Has this
   ever happened to you? Describe the experience.
2. The Prince tells Quinlan that he is a fellow heir to the kingdom as a son of the King. Can you find a Bible verse that tells
   us something similar?

3. Which Bible verse affirms the Prince's words, "Be strong, for I am strong in you"?

CHAPTER 19

1. In chapter 17, we learned that the penthomoth represents passion. Why does passion for Jesus sometimes seem "ugly" to the rest of the world?

CHAPTER 20

1. Quinlan finds Drake instructing children at the haven. Can you find the verse in Scripture where Jesus talks about children's place in the kingdom of heaven?

CHAPTER 21

1. Quinlan tries to warn the prefect of Burkfield about the coming attack on the city, but the prefect doesn't believe him. How is this similar to what Christians often face?

CHAPTER 22

1. This chapter is titled "A Roaring Lion." Can you find a Bible verse that refers to Satan as a roaring lion? According to this verse, what is Satan's objective?

CHAPTER 23

1. At Quinlan's invitation, a knight chose to get free of her paytha. How is this scene similar to what one might experience in reality when a person chooses to be free from a vice or stronghold?

2. Tav was once again unwilling to give up the paytha that had drawn him away from the haven and ultimately from the Prince. Can you find a story in the Bible in which a man walked away from Jesus because of a stronghold in his life?

3. Kalil defeats and destroys the paythas. What might this represent?

4. Thousands of Knights of the Prince come together to fight for Burkfield. What does this represent in the spiritual realm?

CHAPTER 24

1. Silent Warriors (angels) come to the aid of the Knights of the Prince who are fighting for Burkfield. What roles have angels played in Scripture? (For example, the angel who told Mary she would give birth to Jesus was playing the role of messenger.)

EPILOGUE

1. Jesus has some grave words for those who don't truly serve Him in heart. Find the passage in Matthew that describes what Tav experiences when he goes to meet the Prince at the docks.

ANSWERS TO
DISCUSSION QUESTIONS

Answers to Review Questions from the Kingdom Series

1. The Prince represents Jesus Christ.
2. The Knights of the Prince represent all Christians.
3. Chessington represents Jerusalem, and Arrethtrae represents the whole world (*earth* and *terra* are combined backward to make up this word).
4. The Dark Knight, also referred to as the Dark Lord or Lucius, represents Satan.
5. The Silent Warriors are God's angels, and the Shadow Warriors are Satan's demons.
6. A Vincero Knight is a person who has been personally trained by one of Lucius's Shadow Warriors to spread and cultivate evil. Vincero Knights are ruthless and twisted by the evil that has mentored them. They represent people who are committed to propagating evil in the world, such as murderers, drug dealers, and the like.
7. A haven represents a local church, where believers are trained, discipled, and sent out to share the gospel with others.

Answers to Questions for *Sir Quinlan and the Swords of Valor*

CHAPTER 1
1. Evil is most dangerous when we don't recognize it as evil. The Bible says that Satan can appear as an angel of light (2 Corinthians 11:14).

CHAPTER 2

1. Rearrange the letters of *paytha* and you get *apathy.* The diction-
   ary defines *apathy* as a state of indifference, a lack of interest or
   concern, or a lack of emotion or feeling.

2. Apathy, or any vice for that matter, can grow as "large" as we
   allow it. The more we give in to a stronghold, the more control
   it gains over our lives. It's important to remember that the only
   power Satan or his demons have over Christians is the power
   we relinquish to them.

3. The world and the kingdom of God are not compatible, so we
   must give up one to gain the other. The merchant's offer represents the temptation to give up a portion of our spiritual walk
   with the Lord to enjoy something of the world.

4. The shield represents faith, which is our defensive weapon
   against the "fiery darts" of the Evil One. By trading his shield,
   Tav makes himself vulnerable to the attacks of Lucius (Satan).

CHAPTER 3

1. Disty and Bli represent the spiritual *dis*tractions and spiritual
   *bli*ndness that may cause apathy to take root in a person's life.
   Unless a person can see the danger, he or she won't be concerned with it.

2. Apathy can be contagious! When one friend grows apathetic,
   other friends may become apathetic too. When a leader grows
   apathetic, so will many of those over whom he or she has
   influence.

CHAPTER 4

1. Some possibilities are Matthew 10:38; Mark 10:23; Luke
   14:26–27; and Romans 12:1–2.

CHAPTER 5

1. Bli understood he might lose control of Quinlan. A vice like apathy is hard to break because our flesh wars with our spirit. Satan

and his demons will also tempt us to keep a vice in our lives that controls us and keeps us from living a victorious life for Jesus.

2. Lucius didn't want Quinlan to become an active soldier for the King, just as Satan doesn't want a believer to become an active Christian.

3. Some examples are Ecclesiastes 4:8–12; John 17:21–23; 1 Corinthians 12:12–27; and Ephesians 4:11–16.

CHAPTER 6

1. God often calls the "least of the least" to perform amazing works for Him. He does this to show mankind that He is powerful and that "no flesh should glory in His presence" (1 Corinthians 1:25–29). Some biblical examples are Moses, Saul, David, Gideon, most of the disciples, and so on.

2. These things represent the Bible, which is God's Word (Ephesians 6:17).

3. Worldly distractions—material possessions, relationships, pastimes, and so on—can hinder a believer's ability to identify the spiritual battle waging around us (Mark 4:18–19).

4. Possible answers are prayer, financial help, encouragement, and so on.

5. Examples are 1 Thessalonians 5:19 and Hebrews 3:7–12.

CHAPTER 7

1. The sword of God's Word is "living and powerful" (Hebrews 4:12). The better we know it, the better able we are to defend ourselves against arguments and attacks that discourage us and weaken our effectiveness. Jesus gave us an excellent example of how to defend ourselves when He fought His great spiritual battle with Satan in the wilderness. He quoted Scripture for each of Satan's three temptations (Matthew 4:1–11).

CHAPTER 8

1. Because of sin, the world is in decay, and tragedies are a natural result. However, God says He will never leave nor forsake those

who are His (Hebrews 13:5) and that He will work all things for good to those who love Him (Romans 8:28). The final outcome of a tragedy is really dependent on whether the person chooses to believe and follow God—and the good outcome might not be apparent until heaven.

CHAPTER 9

1. Answers will vary.

CHAPTER 10

1. Answers will vary.

CHAPTER 11

1. Just as in Jesus' parable of the sower (Matthew 13:3–8, 18–23), Tav lets the seeds of doubt and unbelief sown by the Evil One take root in his life. Instead of refuting them with truth, he allows the lies to linger so long that he begins to believe them.
2. The verse is Philippians 3:13–14.

CHAPTER 12

1. God's Word and the Holy Spirit are our windows into spiritual realities.

CHAPTER 13

1. One possibility is fasting, described in Matthew 4:1–11; Matthew 17:19–21; Acts 10:30; and Acts 13:2.
2. First Corinthians 6:11 says that through Christ we "were sanctified"—made perfect. That's past tense—we already are who we hope to become! See also Hebrews 10:10–14.
3. We find out who we are in Christ by reading the Bible and spending time with the Lord in prayer. The more we get to know who He is, the more we understand who we are in Him. This is important because our corrupted flesh is in a battle with our perfect spirit (1 Peter 2:11 and Romans 8:1–14), and sometimes that battle keeps us from remembering that

we are more than conquerors (even over our own flesh) in
Christ (Romans 8:37).

4. This theme is explored in the book of Hebrews.

CHAPTER 14

1. This refers to the coming of a "beast" or "antichrist" (false mes-
siah) to rule the earth. Scriptural references include Daniel 7;
2 Thessalonians 2; 1 John 2 and 4; 2 John; and Revelation
13–14, 16–18.

CHAPTER 15

1. God created all people in the first place so that He could have a
relationship with us. Second Peter 3:9 makes it clear that He
doesn't want any of us to perish but desires that we all should
come to salvation through Jesus.

CHAPTERS 16 AND 17

1. The Greek word *pentho* means "passion." The penthomoth represents passion (energetic commitment) as opposed to apathy
(indifference).

2. Passion can be dangerous if misdirected. The difference lies in
the *object* of the passion. Passionate commitment to the cause
of Christ is what moves His kingdom forward.

CHAPTER 18

1. Answers will vary.
2. A good Scripture passage is Romans 8:16–17.
3. See Philippians 4:13.

CHAPTER 19

1. Because passion for Christ offends them just as Jesus said it
would in John 15:18–19.

CHAPTER 20

1. See Matthew 19:14.

CHAPTER 21

1. Often, the unsaved do not believe that their eternal lives are at stake and will not listen to the truth of their need for salvation. This can be frustrating for Christians. We must remember, however, that we are called simply to proclaim the gospel. We are not responsible for whether another person accepts or rejects Jesus.

CHAPTER 22

1. First Peter 5:8 refers to Satan as a roaring lion. His objective is to "devour" and destroy the unwary.

CHAPTER 23

1. Strongholds can have a powerful grip on people, including believers, and can be difficult to give up. Release from a vice or stronghold often requires the accountability and support of strong, faithful friends.
2. The rich young ruler (Matthew 19:16–26; Mark 10:17–27; Luke 18:18–29) is a good example.
3. A passion for serving the Lord is the key to overcoming apathy.
4. It represents Christians joining together in intercessory prayer. (Other answers are possible.)

CHAPTER 24

1. Answers will vary. Some possible roles are that of messenger (those who spoke to Daniel, Mary, Joseph), protector (those who helped Peter, John, Paul), worshiper (those described in Isaiah), proclaimer (as in Matthew, Jesus' birth), minister or caregiver (Elijah, Matthew, Jesus), and warrior (Michael in Revelation 12:7 and Daniel 10:13).

EPILOGUE

1. A similar scene is described in Matthew 7:21–23.

Ride of the Valiant

Emily Elizabeth Black

Ride of the Valiant

AUTHOR COMMENTARY

Apathy is one of the deadliest sins. The Lord has strong words of warning for believers who fall into a lifestyle of apathetic behavior. Apathy spreads to others and hinders God's work. It also destroys the witness of a believer by demonstrating to the rest of the world that God's people appear to be no different than anyone else.

One might think the cause of apathy is laziness, and that is sometimes true. But apathy more often results from spiritual blindness and worldly distraction. One of the most frustrating challenges for a parent, teacher, or pastor is to motivate young people out of apathy and into a vibrant and productive Christian walk. *Sir Quinlan and the Swords of Valor* attempts to accomplish this by showing the contrast between two knights who choose different paths—one of apathy and one of purpose. There is great reward both here and in heaven for those who choose to live a life of purpose for Jesus Christ. It is my heart that this book will encourage people of all ages to live such a life.

♛ ♛ ♛

I know thy works, that thou art neither cold nor hot:
I would thou wert cold or hot. So then because thou
art lukewarm…I will spue thee out of my mouth.
Because thou sayest, I am rich, and increased with
goods, and have need of nothing; and knowest not
that thou art wretched, and miserable, and poor, and
blind, and naked: I counsel thee to buy of me gold
tried in the fire, that thou mayest be rich; and white
raiment, that thou mayest be clothed, and that the
shame of thy nakedness do not appear; and anoint
thine eyes with eyesalve, that thou mayest see. As
many as I love, I rebuke and chasten: be zealous
therefore, and repent. Behold, I stand at the door,
and knock: if any man hear my voice, and open the
door, I will come in to him, and will sup with him,
and he with me.

—REVELATION 3:15–20, KJV

> *"A Pilgrim's Progress for the xbox generation!"*
> —Dave Jackson,
> author of the Trailblazer novels

DISCOVER THE ULTIMATE BATTLE BETWEEN GOOD AND EVIL

Discover a land of swords and battles—where Good and Evil clash, and knights find courage, faith, and loyalty stand tall in the face of opposition. An allegorical medieval re-telling of the Bible from Genesis to Revelation, this captivating series will take you on an adventure you'll never forget! *Kingdom's Dawn, Kingdom's Hope, Kingdom's Edge, Kingdom's Call, Kingdom's Quest,* and *Kingdom's Reign*.

ONLY LOYALTY TO THE KING CAN BRING VICTORY!

Journey to Arrethtrae as the Knights of the Prince await His triumphant return—and with noble hearts live and die in loyal service to the King and the Prince. Follow the exciting adventures of these mighty knights in: *Sir Kendrick and the Castle of Bel Lione, Sir Bentley and Holbrook Court, Sir Dalton and the Shadow Heart* and *Lady Carliss and the Waters of Moorue*.